Mothers, Daughters, Sisters, Wives

Praise for *Mothers, Daughters, Sisters, Wives*

"Karen Rosenbaum is the daughter of division—her father Jewish, her mother Mormon. This two-sidedness shows in her work. Very intelligent and observant, Rosenbaum writes in a way that pulls at your heart and mind and your beliefs. A fine, fine writer and thinker."

—Phyllis Barber, author of *Parting the Veil: Stories from a Mormon Imagination*

"Karen Rosenbaum has been a consistent source of excellent short stories for over forty years, but now we see her genius for character and relationship extends to longer forms as well. Although each story in this collection can be enjoyed on its own, the tapestry they weave together captures the full breadth of families, generation by generation, kindness by kindness, heartache by heartache."

—Eric Jepson, blogger and author of *BYUCK*

"Karen Rosenbaum is a master of the short story, and this collection showcases her very best work. Her prose is elegant, and her stories are constructed with care, but beyond her technical skill, Rosenbaum writes with a wisdom and kindness that binds readers to her characters. The mothers, daughters, sisters, and wives in this collection, as well as all the men who surround them, will linger in your imagination long after you finish the book."

—Angela Hallstrom, author and editor of *Dispensation: Latter-Day Fiction*

"Karen Rosenbaum has a gift for peeling back the layers of death to find the core of life, the layers of dying to find the victory of valiance, the layers of experience to find the triumph of memory. Threads of joy are woven through sorrow to create those unpredictable moments that—for lack of a better term—we call wisdom. These stories sink deep and rise high. And along the way, they gleam with love."

—Lavina Fielding Anderson, author and editor of *Lucy's Book: A Critical Edition of Lucy Mack Smith's Family Memoir*

"To read Karen Rosenbaum's work is to read the backbone of Mormon literature: the vertebrae fashioned to provide not just strength, but flexibility. You can feel it in every precise word, every poised sentence, every assured story. Thoughtful Mormons will be nourished by the fruits of Karen's forty-year labor of love."

—Stephen Carter, author and editor of *Sunstone*

"I am happy to see this collection of stories by Karen Rosenbaum. It is the culmination of a fruitful, lifelong avocation on her part, the writing of succinct yet carefully detailed studies of women. Rosenbaum probes the feminine soul with deep empathy."

—Levi S. Peterson, author of *The Backslider*

Mothers, Daughters, Sisters, Wives

stories by
Karen Rosenbaum

ZARAHEMLA BOOKS

"Burial Places," "The Price of Ties," and "Immersions" have been published, in slightly different forms, in *Exponent II.*
"Paradise Paved" and "Mothers and Daughters" have been published in *Sunstone.*
"Aunt Charlotte's Secrets" has been published in *Irreantum.*
"Long Divisions," "Havesu," "Out of the Woods," "Requiem in L Minor, " and "Acute Distress, Intensive Care" have been published in *Dialogue: A Journal of Mormon Thought.*
"Out of the Woods" was anthologized in *Dispensation: Latter-day Fiction* (Zarahemla, 2010, ed., Angela Hallstrom).

Cover designed by Jason Robinson
Design and layout by Marny K. Parkin

ISBN 978-0-9883233-6-0

Printed in the U.S.A.

Published by:
Zarahemla Books
869 East 2680 North
Provo, UT 84604
info@zarahemlabooks.com
ZarahemlaBooks.com

For my grandmothers,
Ruchel Greenblatt Rosenbaum
and
Karen Elizabeth Christensen Fredrickson,

and

my mother,
Greta Fredrickson Rosenbaum

Contents

Maren

Burial Places

Aw, you just missed 'em," aunt ruth ann said after she kissed Mom and Dad and gave Maren a hug. "The kids went with Gus to put gasoline in the jeep. Then they were goin' over to the stable to feed the horses." Aunt Ruth Ann poured big glasses of green punch, then wiped her hands on her apron. "It's a shame you didn't get here a little sooner."

Gulping down her punch, Maren left the grown-ups in the kitchen and wandered out back to check on the rabbits. Then she lay on her stomach in the clover under the kitchen window. She could hear Aunt Ruth Ann and Mom talking while they were tying bouquets and boxing fruit bottles. Dad would be making little tags so they'd get the right bouquet on the right grave. When everyone was ready, Maren would get to ride to the cemeteries in Uncle Gus's jeep with Len and Jill and all the flowers. Mom and Dad would pick up Grandpa and Aunt Carrie in the Oldsmobile, and Aunt Ruth Ann would go get the great uncles and aunts in her Ford.

Maren reached for a few dandelions. "At least she passed easy," Aunt Ruth Ann was saying.

"It's been eight and a half months," said Mom, "and I remember it clear as if it was today. I'll never forget it."

"You don't forget. You don't ever forget when it's your own close kin. Most especially your mother."

"I was coming up on the bus to see her. Remember?"

"And I had you paged at the station in Salt Lake before you left."

"There I was on the bus, all alone, looking out the window and not seeing anything. I don't ever want to live over those two hours again."

"No worry there," said Dad. "You don't get to live over any hours again."

"Oh, Willy," Mom said. "Now where's that girl?" She came to the window. "Maren!"

Maren roused herself and sat up. "Out here," she called. "Just waitin'." She looped a dandelion chain around her wrist and examined a scab on her knee.

"We bought a big plot," Aunt Ruth Ann was saying. "There's room for all of us."

"No thank you," said Dad. "I don't want to have my remains a-moldering away in the earth. I'm going to be cremated. Dinah can be buried there if she wants to."

"Willy!" Aunt Ruth Ann was cross. "Only pagans get cremated. Dinah, you gonna let him turn to ashes?"

"It's up to him. I don't have any say in it."

"You do if you live longer than he does. Willy, don't you know you won't have a body to be resurrected in if you burn it all up?"

"Huh," Dad said. "What do you think is left of you after you've been underground a year?"

"Shh," Mom whispered. "Maren's out there."

Dad didn't lower his voice. "She knows all about it. She went and dug up her hamster last summer. Kids start out smart. They have to learn to be stupid."

"Well, *hamsters* aren't resurrected." Aunt Ruth Ann sounded sure.

"Who says?"

"Everyone ready?" It was Uncle Gus's voice. Maren hadn't heard the jeep. She stuffed the dandelion chain into her shorts pocket, rolled to her feet, and raced around the side of the house. Jill waved. Her legs dangled over the back license plate. Len was sitting in the driver's seat. He had on a red and white baseball cap, and he lifted it off by the bill and blew inside.

"Pa let me drive," he bragged.

"Aw, he did not," said Maren. "You're only 13."

"He did too."

"Did he, Jill?"

"I wouldn't know," said Jill. "I didn't notice."

"You kids corpses?" Uncle Gus was carrying a box of fruit jars towards the jeep. Uncle Gus had a limp he got in Guam in the war. "Go get some boo*kets*."

"Bouquets, Pa!" said Jill.

"Boo*kets*, Jill," said Uncle Gus.

Maren tugged on his sleeve. "Did you let Len drive?"

"Don't you worry your head, little lady," he said. "Just go get some flowers."

Maren and Jill sat in the back of the jeep to make sure none of the bouquets fell onto the road. Under the damp blanket, the flowers were sweet smelling and pretty. Maren peeked at them and sniffed. Jill slid over closer to her. Jill smelled spicy and sweet, like the snapdragons. "You got any boyfriends?" she asked.

"No." Maren stared at her. "Do *you*?"

"Of course. All the girls in the fifth grade have boyfriends."

"They do?" Maren swallowed. "Who's your boyfriend?"

"Eddie Werner." Jill's fingernails and toenails were bright pink.

Maren looked at her own fingernails, uncolored except for green dandelion stains. She had on Keds, not sandals, but inside the Keds, her toenails were plain too. She looked back over at Jill. "What do you do with him? This Eddie."

"Just things," Jill said. "He gave me this." She pulled out the collar of her blouse and showed off a poodle pin with red rhinestone eyes. "Don't you know any boys?"

"Sure," Maren said. "I mean in the fourth grade there are boys. But they're just boys."

"Wait till the fifth grade." Jill fingered her pin. "That's when you get boyfriends."

The girls slid off the jeep at the Logan Cemetery. Mom and Aunt Ruth Ann sorted through the flowers while Aunt Carrie fanned herself with a *Photoplay* magazine and the great-aunts emerged like moths out of their backseat cocoons. The biggest bouquet was for Grandma's grave. Mom grasped Maren's hand and led the way to the marker. Maren tried to wriggle loose. Jill checked her face in the jeep side mirror and then walked towards them, one foot placed carefully in front of the other like a ballerina Maren had seen once in the *Nutcracker*. Aunt Ruth Ann had hold of Grandpa's elbow.

"Think about Grandma now," Mom said. She sighed. "She loved you very much. How she would have wanted to see you grow up." She wiped her cheek with the back of her free hand.

Maren wasn't sure she wanted to think of Grandma. How did spirits work, anyway? Did they swoop around keeping an eye on their grandchildren? Could Grandma see her when she stole sugar cubes out of the pantry and cherries off Mrs. Albert's tree? Did Grandma know what she was thinking?

Dad brought a fruit jar that he'd filled up with water from a tap, and Mom let go of Maren to put the flowers in the jar. The grave marker was a book with two open pages. On one page was printed Grandma's name, Anna Maren Mikelsen Jensen, then June 14, 1878—her birthdate, then September 9, 1950. Maren remembered. She'd just started the fourth grade. Dad wrote Mrs. Fielding a note so she could miss two days of school, and they drove straight up to Logan. Mom was already there.

On the other gravestone page was Grandpa's name, Alfred George Jensen, and just one date, March 5, 1888. The bottom was empty. "You're her youngest grandchild," said Mom. She squeezed Maren and whispered, "The last and the best."

Grandma had been little for an old person, and she had worn navy blue hats and brooches and dresses that came way down her legs and she had smelled like powder. In the casket she had on a white dress, her temple dress, Mom had said, and her wrinkled cheeks had been rouged the way they were in real life. Now, according to Dad, she'd be all crumbly and dark.

Grandpa was dressed up as if he were going to church, the way he was at the funeral. Usually he wore overalls. Now he took off his hat and knelt down by the marker. He brushed off a few leaves. Aunt Ruth Ann helped him get back up again. "Annie was a great lady," said one of the great-uncles, Moroni or Moses, Maren couldn't keep them straight. "It was 'count of her we could go to school," said the other one. "Her and that old treadle," said the first great-uncle. Everyone was quiet for a minute or two.

"Now for Herb." Mom cleared her throat and wiped her other cheek. Herb was Aunt Carrie's last husband. He had died way before Grandma, of a heart attack. Maren remembered Uncle Herb. His stomach had hung out over his trousers—a beer belly, they'd called it, even if he didn't drink beer.

"Over here," said Dad. He thought it was funny that Aunt Carrie couldn't find Herb's grave herself. Aunt Carrie was Mom and Aunt Ruth Ann's oldest sister, and she dyed her hair and wore shoes with pointy heels. Mom and Aunt Ruth Ann were always exchanging looks behind her back. She had never learned to drive so she never came to the cemetery by herself. There was a double marker over Uncle Herb's grave too, but nothing was written on Aunt Carrie's side.

"Are you going to put your name and birthday here?" Maren asked.

"Not till I'm gone," Aunt Carrie said, "and then just my name and the date I go." She winked at Maren. "It's nobody's business how old I am. Besides, I've been thinking"—she smoothed back her straw-colored hair and her big earring hoops bumped her neck—"maybe I'd rather be buried next to Jasper."

"Jasper!" hooted Dad. They trooped through the markers carrying Uncle Jasper's flowers. Aunt Carrie could never find that grave either. It was about a block from Uncle Herb's.

"Jasper wasn't a good husband to you." Aunt Ruth Ann had hold of Aunt Carrie's elbow now. Aunt Carrie had divorced

Uncle Jasper years ago, before Maren was even born, but she'd heard them talk one night about how he'd been killed in a fight with another man. There was just one small, flat marker on Uncle Jasper's grave, and Aunt Carrie knelt down and put a jar of flowers on it.

"He was the father of my children." Aunt Carrie arranged the flowers.

"And where are her children now?" hissed Aunt Ruth Ann to Mom. Aunt Carrie's son Darrell was in the Navy, but Mom and Aunt Ruth Ann had done some whispering about him before he went. They said Aunt Carrie's daughter Lila lived off in California with her husband and almost never came home.

"I should think you'd want to be buried next to Herb," Mom said. "He did more raisin' of Darrell and Lila than Jasper did."

"I don't know." Aunt Carrie stood up, wobbling a little on her pointy heels and looking at the grave.

Great-aunt Alma was fixing flowers back by the cars. "Lookit here!" she called. "No one has been watchin' after Louise and Frank." She motioned towards the weedy grave.

"And depend on Amy and Lou to not even show up today," said Aunt Ruth Ann.

"We've got extra flowers." Mom headed towards the jeep. "We've got enough to leave Frank and Louise some." Maren stole a glance at Len, who hadn't bothered to get out of the front seat. He looked as if he were sleeping, his cap pulled over his face. She bet he was wide awake.

She didn't say anything as the jeep bounced along the bumpy road to Smithfield. She stroked her legs, already brown though school had just let out for the summer and she hadn't started going to the park yet. She thought about boys. Who could be her boyfriend? Michael Denney was kind of nice. He was about the only boy in the class who was taller than she was. She was tall, Mom said, because Dad was so tall. She was taller than Jill even if Jill was a year and a half older. Her friend Sandra said that

Jimmy Whitlock liked her, but Jimmy Whitlock was little and fat and always wore striped t-shirts. She couldn't have Jimmy Whitlock for a boyfriend. She wanted a boyfriend who looked like Len. Len was tall but not so chunky as Michael Denney. Len walked like a cowboy. Maybe she could find a boyfriend from the sixth grade. Jill would be impressed by that.

Jill poked her. "I know where babies come from," she whispered.

"I do too," Maren said.

"Where?'

"From mothers' tummies."

"They don't come from tummies," said Jill scornfully. "They come from uteruses."

"Well, down there by tummies," Maren said.

"Do you know how it happens?"

Maren repeated what Mom had told her. "The husband plants a seed in the wife . . . ."

"It doesn't have to be the husband," Jill laughed. "It could be any man. Or any boy after he's 14."

"Not just the husband?"

"Shh!" Jill said. They both looked over their shoulders. Len was leaning over the back of his seat. "Turn around, smarty," Jill told him. He snickered, but he turned around. Jill paused. "And do you know how the man plants the seed?"

Maren was silent. That part of the explanation had not been very clear. Mom hadn't seemed to want to talk about it very long. "How do *you* know?" she asked.

"I'm almost eleven," said Jill.

The jeep jolted to a stop. Jill whispered, "I'll tell you tonight." The great-grandparents on Grandma's side were buried in Smithfield. Mom and Aunt Ruth Ann and the rest were already there waiting for the flowers. "Got stuck behind that tractor," Uncle Gus grumbled.

"Look how old." Mom pointed out the gravestones to Maren. "You and Jill see if you can find the oldest stone here. We ought to have the names and dates made darker," she said to Aunt Ruth Ann. "They can do that, can't they?"

"This one was born in 1804." Maren traced the numbers with her finger. "And this one was born in 1797!" She heard Jill giggle and looked around. "Where are you?" she shouted. Mom scowled and put her finger to her mouth.

"Try and find me," Jill answered.

Her voice seemed to come from behind the big gravestone, the one that looked like a table, over by the tree. Maren sneaked up and peered around the side. Not there. She raced over to an even bigger stone and then one beyond that. She heard giggling down by the ditch. She crept quietly, making sure she didn't give herself away. She was just about to shout, "Got ya!" when she saw it wasn't Jill at all. It was another girl, an older girl, and she didn't have a blouse on, and a dark-skinned boy was sitting close behind her and unhooking her bra.

Maren swallowed and took a step backwards, just one step. "Maren!" she heard Jill call from over by the big marker. She got just a glimpse of the boy massaging the girl's breasts, and then she turned towards Jill's voice. "Where've you been?" Jill demanded.

"Just lookin' for you."

"Didn't find me though, did ya?"

Maren shook her head.

Back in the jeep, Jill sidled up close to her again. "Do you want a lot of babies when you get married?"

"I don't know," Maren said. "Do you?"

"Yes." Jill began braiding Maren's hair. "I want a lot of babies. Maybe six or seven."

"When do you want to get married?"

"Oh maybe when I'm 17." She pulled the hair tight and Maren winced. "Seventeen sounds like a good age if you're going to have lots of babies. My mom was 19 and she had four babies. Your mom was 27, you know. Maybe that's why she only had you."

"She says she can't have any more."

"That's because she was so old when she got married. Stop wiggling."

"No, it's not." Maren tried to hold still. "She says it's because she has little bumps inside her."

"Well, she probably has the little bumps because she was so old when she got married. There." She finished braiding. "I don't have an elastic though. Can you wear lipstick yet?"

"No," breathed Maren. "Can you?"

"I'm not supposed to, but I have one. See?" She pulled out of her pocket a little gold tube and screwed out the waxy orange stick.

"Can I try some on?"

"Tonight," said Jill.

Grandpa's people were in the Newton cemetery. "Last stop!" Uncle Gus said when he pulled the jeep over under a tree. There were only a few bouquets left. Grandpa and Aunt Ruth Ann were strolling among the graves, pointing at some and talking. Aunt Carrie was sitting in the Oldsmobile with the door open and her bare feet in the grass. Mom and Dad were helping the great-uncles and aunts out of the cars. "Your grandpa probably knows everyone here." Uncle Gus chewed on a twig. Mom said he did that to keep himself from smoking.

"Grandpa!" Jill called. He and Aunt Ruth Ann waited for them. Jill tugged on his thumb. "Grandpa, do you know everyone here?"

"Pretty nearly."

"Who's that?" Jill pointed to a grave at random.

"Anton Rasmussen," said Grandpa promptly. He wagged Maren's new braid, already loosening because they hadn't had a tie.

"Was he your friend?"

"No. He was the father of my friend Hyrum. He's been gone fifty years."

"Fifty-four," Aunt Ruth Ann said, reading the marker through the bottom of her glasses.

"Come on, Maren," said Jill. "Let's go see if the beehives are still here!"

Maren looked down to see a stone lamb curled up atop a tiny marker.

"That's a love baby's grave," Jill explained.

"Oh," Maren said. She decided she wouldn't ask.

The beehives were the same place as last year, by the hole in the fence and the high grass.

Dad was whistling for them to come. Jill picked two daisies and gave one to Maren. "Think of the boy you want for your boyfriend," Jill said, "and see if he loves you." They stretched out in the back of the empty jeep and pulled petals off the daisies. Maren tried to think who could be her boyfriend.

"What were you doin' out there with the birds and bees?" Len flipped a twig at Jill. "Learnin' all about it?"

"Aw, shove off, Len." Jill pulled off the last petal. "He loves me," she said. "How about yours?"

"Mine came out wrong," said Maren, "but it's okay because I don't have anybody yet anyway."

"You will," Jill said, "when you're older." She closed her eyes. Her pale eyelashes almost disappeared against the freckles of her cheek.

Dad waved as he got into the car next to Aunt Carrie. "See you back at the house, Gus!" he called. The jeep brought up the rear of the caravan leaving the cemetery, but Uncle Gus stopped as the cars went on down the road. He turned around. "Wanna stop at the Dairy Queen?" he asked.

"Yeah!" they said. Even Len said, "Yeah!"

Maren lay back and watched the blue sky. When they got to Uncle Gus's house, Aunt Ruth Ann would feed everybody fried chicken and bottled-pear pie, and the adults would talk about the dead people, and Dad and Uncle Gus would play cribbage in the kitchen. Jill would go across the street to get Arlene and Dennis Sewell and they'd hide from each other in all the big backyards and ditches and sheds, and when it got *really* dark and Aunt Ruth Ann called them in, they'd bring out the Canasta cards and the Monopoly board. But maybe this year Len would think he was too big to play Canasta and Monopoly.

When Mom and Dad went back to Grandpa's, Maren would get to sleep on the second bed in Jill's room, the bed Jill's sister Annie slept in when she lived at home. But first there would be milk and cookies and prayers in the kitchen with Aunt Ruth Ann and Uncle Gus and Len, and then Len would go down to his room in the basement, and Maren and Jill would come upstairs. They'd try on the lipstick in front of Jill's mirror and scrub it all off with cold cream and Kleenexes. They'd turn off the lights when Aunt Ruth Ann would holler at them, and they'd crawl into their beds, but they'd stay awake late talking about boyfriends and babies and how to be beautiful.

The Price of Ties

MAYBE WE SHOULDN'T GO," THE MOTHER SAYS.

The daughter has just splashed a sauce pan full of soapy water on the windshield and is scraping off the bugs with a squeegee. She doesn't look up. "You'll feel bad if we don't."

The mother sighs, a long, perfected, pitiful sigh. "It's three hours to Price and three hours back. You just drove in from Wyoming last night. And you have that ski pain in your rear end."

"Sciatic pain," the daughter says. "I don't have it anymore."

"And Darrell says she doesn't even know him when he comes all the way from Texas. Not that he comes very often. And Lila *never* comes."

"So *we*'ll go." The daughter examines the windshield, then nods. "Maybe it's not for Aunt Carrie. Maybe it's for *us*." She points to the yellow flower on the front of her T-shirt.

The mother regards with dread the door handle of her daughter's car. "Hardly anyone visits her. She just lies there all alone. But I can't drive all that way by myself. I've never driven on freeways."

The daughter sets the empty pot on the porch and wipes her hands on her Levi's. "*I* drive on freeways." She opens the car door for her mother. "It'll be okay. You'll see. And we won't stay long."

The daughter hums as the Honda laps up the Interstate. She likes to drive, likes the sensation of speed and smoothness and control. Her monthly weekend trips from Evanston began when her father was ill and continued after he died. She acknowledges to herself the pleasures of escape. Cleve can manage—Gordy and Madeleine spend Saturdays with him at the store, Tracy has a job at the Dairy Queen. And when they asked her to teach the nine-year-olds, Madeleine's class, at church, she told them yes, of course, one always said yes to church callings, but she had to have one Sunday a month off because she had obligations to her widowed mother—she enunciated the phrase reverently—in Salt Lake City.

The mother proposed the journey to Price four Saturdays before, when she and the daughter were stirring up strawberry jam. The daughter dropped the big wooden spoon and burst out, "Let's, Mom! I want to see her before she dies. You need to see her too."

Immediately the mother looked startled, as if she hadn't been the one to make the suggestion. "I don't know, dear. Maybe it's not such a good idea."

"It is a good idea. We'll go next month. The week before, call the home to let them know we're coming. Okay?"

And so it is that this hot August morning, the Honda is speeding south and the mother is chewing on her lower lip.

"It's more important to see people when they're alive," the daughter wrinkles her nose to adjust her sunglasses, "rather than wait till they're laid out in a coffin."

"Carrie's laid out in a bed. Darrell says she's not really living. Well. Not living the way people live. She's living the way turnips live, I guess."

The daughter laughs for just an instant, then clears her throat. "Sometimes I felt that she was your other child, the way you and Dad took care of her."

"I haven't done anything since your dad passed on. She doesn't even know he's gone. She can't talk on the phone any more. There's not a phone by her bed even if she could talk. I call the staff every week. They always say she's the same, not unconscious, but not really awake either. They say they'll let me know if there's any change. For better or for worse." She smiles wryly. "They didn't seem all that enthusiastic that we're coming."

The daughter snorts. "You'd think they could at least hold a phone up to her ear and let you talk. Maybe she'd hear you." She holds an imaginary phone to her own ear. "Just think, once she was a telephone operator!"

"And when telephone operators were real people, not tinny voices. She knew everybody and everybody's business. If you were trying to reach Irma, she'd tell you that Irma was having her hair done." The mother folds her hands into the lap of her zip-front dress. "Course that was because Dragerton was a little town. She wouldn't have known everybody in Salt Lake."

"She liked coming to Salt Lake."

"After your Uncle Herb died, she spent Christmas and Thanksgiving with us. You remember. And your dad and I were going down there every month until he got sick. He was fixing things for her on that last trip. Furnace filter, I think. He replaced her furnace filter."

"How was she then?" The daughter glances in her rear view mirror, then switches into the faster lane.

"Not quite right in the head. She yelled at me when I tried to toss out all the spoiled stuff in her refrigerator. And newspapers and mail just piled up, but she wouldn't let me go through them. I wonder if she forgot how to read." The mother holds out her hands and examines her thickened fingers. "I called Darrell when we got home, and next thing I knew he'd put her in that home." She makes two fists. "I wouldn't have said anything if I'd known he'd do that. We could've got someone to look in on her, help her."

"Weren't people already looking in on her?"

"She'd made her friends mad. They'd stopped dropping by. She'd accuse them of stealing things." She watches a moving van pull even with the Honda. "This was an awful trip before air-conditioning." She pauses. "She could be downright mean."

"Mean? Aunt Carrie?"

"She was mean to me when we were children. She resented me for being born. You know your grandma had a lot of miscarriages between Carrie and me, and she got used to being an only child. Once she stuck me up on the chicken house roof. When Mama told her to get me down, she asked if she'd get a whipping if she did, and Mama said yes, she'd get a whipping either way, so Carrie said then that I could stay up there all night as far as she was concerned. And she used to pinch me in church, and when Mama made her take me along with her friends, Carrie'd tell me there were snakes hidden everywhere, even under the snow, and they were going to bite me. That's why I'm so scared of snakes to this day."

The daughter chuckles. "Was she mean to Aunt Ruth Ann too?"

"Naw. By the time Ruthie was born, she'd already decided everything was *my* fault. Ruthie was just Carrie's sidekick. I think the first words Carrie taught her were, 'I hate Dinah.' They used to chant that at me, my big sister and my baby sister."

The daughter looks for the exit to Highway 6. "I didn't know that," she says. "That *is* mean."

"At church they make you feel bad if you have just one child, like you're depriving the family of all the blessings of the kingdom, but sometimes I'd think about the way Carrie treated me and I wasn't sorry I couldn't have more."

"I didn't feel deprived," says the daughter. "I felt spoiled."

"You used to ask for a little sister or brother."

"I used to ask for a pony too, didn't I? And of course *I* would have been the mean one if you'd had more kids. I would have been the oldest."

"You wouldn't have been mean." Her voice lacks conviction. "I wasn't mean to my baby sister. My baby sister," the mother repeats. "Ruthie's been gone a year now. When Carrie goes, I'll be the only one left."

"Hardly," the daughter says.

"Of my generation. And all the earlier generations."

"Well." The daughter thinks. "There's Uncle Gus even if he's not blood. And your cousins. Cousins count."

"Yes," the mother admits. "Cousins do count." She purses her lips. "Carrie was mean to your grandpa too."

"No!"

"Remember, she took him so Will and I could take a vacation, and she put him into the hospital when he messed in the bed. I'll never forgive myself for letting her take him. She had no patience, not one whit. He died because he was so miserable in that hospital."

"Mom! He was 92! Even you couldn't keep him alive forever!"

"And she was so stubborn. She smoked up to the minute they hooked her up to oxygen. She would've kept on too, but the doctor told her she'd explode."

The daughter shakes her head. "It's pretty," she says, "the road to Soldier Summit."

The mother looks at the trees. "Are you trying to distract me?"

"Distract *you*?" The daughter laughs. "Aunt Carrie didn't seem to resent you when you were adults."

"No," the mother says finally. "I guess not. Even though then she did have reason. Will made enough money so I never had to work like she did, and we could live in a nice house. Carrie's first husband—you never knew Jasper—he was a drunkard even though he came from good church people and took Carrie to the temple. Your dad wasn't a believer, but he was a mighty good man. Like your Cleve."

"Amen," says the daughter. "And like Uncle Herb."

"Yep. Herb adored Carrie, and he'd have given her the moon. Course he never had the moon to give. You couldn't get rich working in the mines. Most times you couldn't even break even."

"We're getting close to those mines." The daughter points with her chin at the dark hills. The Honda glides through Helper and Carbonville, and the two women are silent, remembering. When they pull into a gas station in Price, a man in overalls points them down the road.

The nursing home looks like a remodeled supermarket faced in gray cinder blocks. The only other vehicle in the visitors' lot is a big brown stationwagon that takes up two spaces. The daughter lets her mother lead the way. Wispy old people in wheelchairs stare at them as they pass through the lobby. One woman's head lolls loosely as if her neck were a coil.

"Don't ever let them put me in a place like this," the mother hisses.

The daughter looks around. "Looks clean enough anyway."

"We're here to see Carrie Egan," the mother says to a woman in a hospital green smock behind the high counter. "I called that we were coming. I'm her sister, and this here is my daughter."

"Room 5," says the woman in green. "First bed."

"Are you the person I talk to on the phone?"

The woman shrugs. "Could be."

"Do you think she'll know us?"

The woman in green shakes her head. "Probably not. She might smile for you. Carrie's a sweetie. She mostly sleeps."

The mother sucks in her breath as they pass through Room 5's open door. The daughter finds her a chair, guides her into it. "Hello, darling," the mother says to the form in the bed. "It's Dinah, dear." Carrie is sleeping on her side, her hands beneath her wrinkled cheek. Under the thin pink blanket, she looks very small.

The daughter slips into another chair and looks around the room. The middle bed is empty, the covers tossed aside. Another old woman is sleeping soundlessly in the bed next to the window.

"Can you hear me, dear?" the mother asks. She reaches out and touches Carrie's forehead.

Carrie opens her eyes. She smiles, a bland, nonspecific smile. She is no longer the aunt of the daughter's past, tall, with straw hair and bangly earrings, wobbling on spiked heels, smoking Lucky Strikes.

"It's Dinah, dear," the mother says again. She takes Carrie's veiny little hand. "We drove down from Salt Lake to see you."

Carrie doesn't seem to focus. Sometimes she looks at her sister, sometimes at the ceiling beyond.

"Will would have liked to come," the mother says. "But he couldn't." Her voice trembles. "Do they treat you well here? Is the food okay?"

Carrie's smile grows wider.

"And the people, the other people." The mother looks at the other beds. "Are the people," she searches for a word, "kind? Are they good to you? That's what's important, that they're good to you." She is squeezing Carrie's hand. "You know I love you, don't you, dear?" She coughs out a tiny laugh. "Remember how when Mama used to spank us, she'd say, 'You know I love you, don't you?'" She puts Carrie's hand down and strokes it. Carrie's eyes close and her breathing is very quiet. The mother speaks slowly. "I love you even if you hated me when I was little. I loved you then too. That's why it hurt so much. You were so strong and talented and beautiful. I was always the runt, the plain one. Even Ruthie grew up to be taller than me."

She sighs. "Ruthie's gone now, Carrie. And Will's gone. They aren't gone forever, just gone on ahead. They're waiting for us, Carrie. Like Herb."

The daughter's eyes are liquidy, but the mother's voice grows stronger and her cheeks are dry. "I just had to come, Carrie," she says, "to tell you I love you. To tell you goodbye." She stands and leans over Carrie and kisses her on the cheek. Then she turns to the daughter, who is wiping her eyes. "Let's go," she says softly. The daughter puts her arm around her mother's shoulder as if she is the strong one.

"Okay," she whispers.

At the door, they turn to look at Carrie. Her eyes are open and she reaches out her hand. "Dinah," she says. Then she closes her eyes again and though they return to take her hand and pat her shoulder and though her breathing seems stronger, she doesn't stir.

"She looks more peaceful," the daughter says finally. This time when they leave the room, no one calls them back.

They slide into a booth at Fay's. "Will and I always brought her here," the mother says.

"Fay was a friend of Carrie's, but I think she sold out and moved to Las Vegas to live with her daughter. I don't know who runs the place now."

"So Carrie knew people in Price too."

"Sure. You had to come to Price all the time if you lived in Dragerton. Wasn't anything in Dragerton but a gas station."

"What did Carrie have when you came here?"

"She always had a hamburger and fries and a piece of peach pie."

"Then," says the daughter, "we'd better do the same."

The fries are limp and cold, and the daughter tries to revive them by soaking them in catsup and Tabasco sauce. "This is how Cleve likes them," she says. "Cold grease."

"I don't guess he's got anymore active in the church?"

"Nope."

"Well, you'll just have to do like me. Wait till he dies and then have all his temple work done for him."

"What is it about the women in our family?" asks the daughter. "Not a believing husband in the whole bunch."

"Well, Gus got to be a high priest. After Ruthie died, he went back to church."

"I think that's just so the widows would take care of him."

The mother takes a bite of her pickle and winces. "Could be."

"Why do men make everything so complicated? Believing isn't the easiest thing in the world for me either, but I decided my kids and I would be better off at church, so I try not to think too hard about all the weird things and I just go."

"You've done good," says the mother. "And Tracy graduated from seminary."

"And I know where she is at night." The daughter looks unhappily at the rest of her hamburger. "I'm not going to be able to finish this," she says. "But you can't count on your kids coming out right even if you send them to church. The bishop's son got arrested for growing marijuana out behind their horse barn. He was selling it to other kids at the high school."

The mother shakes her head. "Most of the time the church helps. Now it didn't help Ruthie in that she died from breast cancer anyway, but Carrie never would've got emphysema if she hadn't smoked all those years. And I think it did something to her brain cells too, the cigarettes. Clogged them up somehow so she couldn't think clear."

The café doesn't have peach pie anymore, so they order apple, but it tastes store-bought, from the freezer. They each eat a few bites, then put down their forks.

"Carrie didn't cook much, did she?" the daughter asks.

"Naw. And she didn't eat right either. Lived on coffee and sweet rolls. And cigarettes." The mother opens her purse and plucks out her wallet. "Will and I would take her canned hams. But vegetables—green, yellow, orange—she said those colors were okay for blouses and trousers, but she wasn't about to put anything like that in her mouth."

"Well," the daughter says, "she's made it to 80."

The mother counts out dollar bills. "Now Carrie was a real Mormon even though she smoked and drank beer and coffee and never went to church and cursed a blue streak."

The daughter raises her eyebrows. "What's a real Mormon then?"

"It's what you are deep down. Not what you do. Once Carrie asked me to do her temple work for her when she was gone."

"What did you say?"

"I said, 'Why don't you do it yourself?' But of course I'll do it for her. It's funny. She said to me, 'Maybe I oughta be sealed to Jasper instead of Herb.' But I'm gonna have her sealed to Herb."

"Do you want to stop by to see her once more? On the way home?"

The mother thinks. "Yes," she says. "Let's."

Carrie doesn't open her eyes this time even though the mother sits and talks with her. In a metal cupboard, the daughter finds a quilt pieced out of men's ties, one of Carrie's own quilts, and she runs her hand over it. She has a similar one at home, on Tracy's bed.

Swinging Carrie's hand, the mother hums "I'm Looking over a Four-leaf Clover" and then "Love at Home." The daughter wanders around the room. The bed in the middle is occupied now, by another sleeping lady, a plump, substantial one. A wheelchair is parked at the bottom of her bed. Finally the mother kisses Carrie again on the cheek, and she and the daughter walk out past the old people sagging in their wheelchairs. A Golden Retriever is lying on the carpet, and it alone raises its head when they pass through the heavy glass doors. The mother lets out a short breath and smiles. "She worked so hard so many years," she says. "Now she rests."

The daughter watches the center line as the Honda speeds up the highway towards the Interstate. The mother dozes a little, then is startled to wakefulness, then dozes again. Carbon County becomes a just a smudge in the rear view mirror.

Mothers and Daughters

Else Pedersen Mikelsen, 12 January 1850–28 May 1920

THE DOCTOR TOLD ANNA THERE WAS NOTHING WRONG with her mother, but all that meant was that there wasn't anything wrong that *he* could see or hear or feel. Her heart was strong, he said, and her lungs sounded clear. When Anna asked her how she felt, she said she didn't hurt particularly, but she was very tired. She was 70. That was enough. She went to bed, in the little bedroom they had made hers, and she just got up to use the toilet, which she only had to do once or twice a day as she ate and drank almost nothing, and one Friday morning Anna, her heart pounding, found her mother twisted like a bent lightning rod on the bedcovers, and she knew at once that it was over.

She straightened her mother's legs and folded the arms across her chest and lay down on the bed next to the body. Alfred was at the farm till tomorrow night, the girls would be up at 6:30, in about half an hour—this was the last day of school before summer, and they would be squabbling and fidgety. Maybe she shouldn't tell them now—but Dinah always came in to kiss her grandmother good-bye before she ran down the street to collect her friends. Carrie and Ruthie, they wouldn't have to know till later. But that was no good—once they saw Anna's face, they'd all know.

She turned on her side and stroked her mother's wrinkly cheek. Yes, tired, Anna thought. Mother worked so hard, and work had hardened her. In Viborg she did factory work, farm work, house work—someone else's house, someone else's farm.

Before she was 20, she had a child, a girl, to raise alone. And then for weeks, on the boat to America, she and little Inger lurched about the steerage. In New York she finally found someone who spoke Danish and who helped them find the train to Utah and the Mormons who knew her parents back in Denmark. She did farm work in Cache Valley too, tying the cut grain into bundles, Inger following along beside her, and she worked in the Andreasens' house in the winter, sewing, cleaning, cooking, Inger playing by herself under the kitchen table. When at last Mother got her own house, she still didn't get her own husband— she had to share him with Aunt Stena, who lived next door. And when the U.S. marshals began arresting polygamists, she had to move her growing brood to the ranch, away from Aunt Stena and the town. Pumping and lugging water, washing clothes and bedding in two big tubs, milking cows, churning butter, carding and weaving wool, sewing clothes and curtains, scrubbing floors with lye, braiding rugs out of rags, making soap, making ludefisk, making five children besides Inger, burying two of those children. No wonder her lips were tight.

Anna sat up and lifted her mother's hand, pressed it to her own lips. She remembered the time, after Father died, when her mother couldn't get out of bed. Sick and exhausted, Mother was trying to run the ranch with Mose and Frank, just boys, and trying to save enough money so Inger could go to college and get a teaching credential. Aunt Stena came and packed Mother with cloths wrung out in hot turpentine water, trying to break the fever. Later, Mother told Anna she had wanted more than anything to sink back and pass away, but she had looked around and counted her children—Frank, the youngest only nine—all weeping around her bed. She knew then she had to fight to live. This spring, Mother had chosen to stop living.

Anna stood up and wiped her eyes with a handkerchief from her apron pocket. Her mother had made that apron, had crocheted that handkerchief. Anna closed her mother's door. In the kitchen she poured oatmeal and water into a pot and called the girls.

Anna's brothers, Frank and Mose, came as soon as she sent for them, and they lifted Mother out of the bed and carried her onto the big dining table. The brothers sat with Anna for a while, then took Mose's car to the cemetery to get things ready there. Mose said he'd get word out to the farm, to Alfred. Not wanting the girls underfoot, Anna shooed them off to school. Only Dinah, her sweet middle child, was teary and hesitant. Carrie and Ruthie had lowered their eyes and quietly left.

It was Anna's job, preparing bodies for burial. Nobody in Logan did it better. She had laid out how many bodies, dozens and dozens, on their own dining room tables, tenderly washing and drying and dressing them. If it was an unexpected death, no burial clothing, she would measure the body and go home and sew the clothes. Now, from the chest at the foot of Mother's bed, she took the burial clothes, all ready. Mother had seen to that.

She looked so small on the table. Inger would be along soon, but Anna had Mother to herself right now, to herself for the last time. She brought water and vinegar and clean rags from the kitchen. She brushed out her mother's long gray hair—long enough to sit on—and braided and coiled it again, a little looser than Mother would have wanted. She put a touch of rouge on the cheeks. Mother would have thought that foolishness, but she looked a little less severe that way.

But no lipstick. Maybe because English wasn't her native tongue, Mother hadn't talked very much. Sometimes she had seemed about to speak, but then she would press her lips tighter together. Anna wondered about Inger's father back in Viborg and why her mother hadn't married him. And their own father, here—why *did* she marry him when he already had a wife. And what had been going on in her mind these past months as she lay all those hours in bed? Anna kissed her mother's forehead. Her mother loved them all. Her children, grandchildren. She adored

Dinah especially and even in these last numb months kept white peppermints under her pillow for her favorite grandchild. But as much as Mother had cared for them, she wanted even more to leave them. Anna wiped her eyes. Was it really better where Mother was now?

Father had been gone 28 years—blood poisoning, at 62, from a splinter of a fence post embedded in his arm. He was a distant, decent man, who provided well for both his families, but any passion he had he must have spent on his first wife, the young one who died in childbirth two years after he brought her here from Alborg. Anna figured he took his next two wives, the polygamous ones, as a duty. Neither Mother nor Aunt Stena seemed to mourn his death. After he died, Anna had heard Aunt Stena whisper to Mother, "I'm so glad it wasn't you, my dear. I can live without him easier than I could without you." There, beyond the dining room table, on the wall above the china cabinet, was the photograph—Father seated between Mother and Aunt Stena, the children arranged like flowers around them. No one was smiling. Sometimes Mother and Aunt Stena would talk in Danish, sometimes in English. Mother *had* mourned when Aunt Stena died, of spotted fever, at 59. Anna calculated the years. That was close to two decades ago.

Anna held her mother's cold, small, bare hand. Mother never wore a wedding ring. On Anna's hand was the fat gold band that Alfred got from Needham's up on North Main. That ring was nineteen years old, but shiny still. She heard Inger coming up the front steps. She leaned over and kissed Mother's cheek. There was such a lot still to do.

Anna Maren Mikelsen Jensen, 14 June 1878–9 September 1950

DINAH WAS GRATEFUL THAT NO ONE HAD CHOSEN TO SLIDE in next to her on the Greyhound bus. She had put her big bag with the bottled apricots and wax-paper-wrapped cookies—oatmeal, her mother's favorites—on the empty seat. Her magazines were in there too, but she didn't pull them out to read. Instead she stared out the window, sometimes leaning her forehead against the glass, sometimes wiping her eyes and cheeks with Kleenexes from her jacket pockets.

Will had dropped her off early at the bus station, then had planned to take Maren over to his sister's house for the weekend. That meant no one had been home when Ruthie tried to reach them there, so she had called at the bus station and had them page her. Dinah had shuddered when she heard her name called over the loudspeaker.

"Mama's gone," Ruthie had said over the station's office telephone. "I thought you should know before you got here. Maybe you want Will to drive you instead of taking the bus."

Dinah had clutched the receiver and swallowed hard. "Dinah?" Ruthie cleared her throat. "Are you still there?"

"Did she pass easy?" Dinah asked.

"Pretty easy. Daddy called me at seven, and I got there about seven-thirty. She wasn't really asleep, but not really awake either. She was breathing funny. Daddy was holding her hand. Then I could tell she wasn't breathing any longer, and I told him she'd left us. We both sat there and then I remembered I should try to get hold of you before you left Salt Lake. Daddy's out in his shop. I think he wants to be alone."

"I'll come ahead on the bus," Dinah said. "Pick me up at the usual time." She gave Ruthie the phone number for Will's sister, so Will could call Logan as soon as he heard. Then she hung up.

"I'm sorry," the lady in the station office said in a trembly voice. "I know how hard it is to lose your mother."

Everyone in the station seemed to know. The driver smiled sadly at her when he put her suitcase in the cargo bin. The other passengers looked concerned when she climbed on the bus. As soon as she was seated, the door closed, and the engine moved from neutral into gear. They must have been waiting for her.

The route from Salt Lake to Ogden was never pretty, but she let her mind move along the power lines and railroad tracks and truck stops and the factories. After Brigham City, she melted into the canyons, the green hills and valleys, a few trees already yellow. Farm houses, barns, small fenced pastures. Horses. You snapped your thumb into the palm of your other hand if you saw a white horse, and if you saw three white horses in a single day, you'd have good luck.

Mama had taught her that.

Mama. Dinah felt like an orphan.

She'd been coming on the bus one weekend every month for a year now, ever since Mama got the cancer. She and Will and their Maren drove the Pontiac up for holidays and birthdays. Of course Ruthie had had most of the responsibility since she was the one who lived close by, right in Logan. Daddy could do the basic stuff, even learned how to use the washer, but Mama cussed him when he tried to do anything in the kitchen. Dinah had started seeing them as old, helpless. And Salt Lake seemed so far away.

Before she got sick, Mama had taken care of everybody. It was always that way. Mama had told her that before she and Daddy got married, she was the one who stayed with her big sister Inger when she had her babies, and when Inger's daughter had her children, even Dinah could remember, it was Mama, not Inger, that she called. Mama, not Inger, took care of Grandma before and after she decided to die. And when Dinah's own big sister Carrie cut off her finger in the mower up at the farm, Mama knew to scorch a cloth with the iron and put in little sticks for splints and push the finger back on and pour table salt around it and bind it tight with a string. When they got into town, the doctor saw that the tip of the finger was pink and said he couldn't have done a better job himself. And afterwards, Carrie could play the piano with all her fingers.

They'd have to plan the funeral, she and Ruthie. Carrie didn't play the piano anymore, but her son Darrell played the violin, and maybe Ruthie's Annie could sing between a couple of the talks. Mama would approve of that. Their cousin Oscar was a bishop in Idaho. He could be the final speaker. What were Mama's favorite hymns? Daddy would know. "God Be with You Till We Meet Again." That was Dinah's own favorite. Someone should tell about Mama and her sewing machine. How she made all the costumes for the float for the Pioneer Day parade and how she sewed all those pretty dresses for her and Carrie and Ruthie and their cousins too. And the granddaughters. That last dress she made for Maren though, the colors were funny. Her eyesight had started to go. Maybe they should sing one of those work hymns at the funeral, maybe "Put Your Shoulder to the Wheel." Will always made fun of that one.

Will didn't believe all the stuff she believed. He didn't ever go to church, except for funerals and once when Maren was giving a two-and-a-half-minute talk. But he was a good man. Mama said so. Of course, Will was a saint compared to Carrie's first husband. And both Mama and Daddy had preferred him to Ruthie's Gus too. Not one of their sons-in-law turned out to be what Carrie called a temple-trottin' Mormon. But Will at least didn't smoke. And he helped Daddy build things like that wall in front of the creek and the banister and new steps on the porch.

The countryside outside the bus window was blurred now. It was her glasses. She'd steamed up her glasses with her tears. "Where are you right now, Mama?" Dinah thought. "Are you looking down on me like an angel? Or maybe you're in the workshop with Daddy. Is it breaking your heart to see us weep?"

She snapped her thumb into her palm for the second white horse.

Dinah Else Jensen Daynes, 22 March 1912–1 October 2005

EVERY SINGLE MORNING MAREN WOKE AT FOUR AND JUST lay there, staring at the dark ceiling and thinking about Mom over there in the nursing home. Beside her Cleve would be rumbling softly—he snored when he slept on his back. How she envied him that gift of sleep. Maybe Mom would be staring at the ceiling now too. There were lights on in the hall outside her room, so her ceiling wouldn't be dark.

When Maren got there early, before the aides had Mom washed and dressed, sometimes her watery eyes would be open and focused far away. Maren wondered what her mother was thinking, what she remembered. Usually, though, Mom was up, in her wheelchair. Sometimes she'd be peering at her arthritic hands, pulling on her fingers as if trying to straighten them. Sometimes she'd be gazing at the television—nature shows or puppet programs, her breakfast tray beside her. Sometimes she'd already be in one of the activities—gardening meant putting plants in pots, baking meant stirring dough or watching April, the activities lady, whip up some cupcakes. Maren would sit beside Mom and help. Those days Mom would brighten when Maren came into the room and put her face up to be kissed. "Hello doll," she would say. Or she'd chatter, "Uncle Mose and Aunt Ada came to see me yesterday. Wish you'da been here." Maren had been there. And Uncle Mose and Aunt Ada had been dead for more than 50 years.

And then there were the awful days when Mom was livid and would call the aides words Maren didn't know Mom even knew or the even worse days when she was sulky and wouldn't talk at all except maybe to hiss, "I wouldn't treat a dog the way you treat me." Once, years after Aunt Carrie died, her son Darrell came to visit Mom. Mom was in one of her nasty moods and she snapped at Darrell, and he just laughed, and said, "The old girl has some fight in her still."

Maren spent a lot of time forgiving herself. She didn't have a choice, she said, and her friends and her cousins agreed. She'd managed to keep Mom in her own home in Salt Lake for two years after the stroke. She found three good women who stayed with her, alternating days and nights so she was never alone. But there were the phone calls in the middle of the night, and what could Maren do—Evanston was almost two hours away and that was if she drove fast and the roads were clear. As it was, she was driving to Salt Lake three or four times a month. She wasn't working anymore, except sometimes to do books for Cleve at the store, but she was trying to help Maddy out, getting the twins to their lessons a couple of days a week, and Cleve's parents were starting to fail. And the orthopedist said it was only a matter of time before Maren needed to have that knee replaced. So they'd lied and told Mom it would just be for a little while that she'd be staying in the nursing home in Evanston. It had been close to two years now.

And then *this* morning, the phone started that awful song, the one Cleve had put on it, and Maren sat up, grabbed the receiver, and took it out in the hall.

"Mrs. Gledhill," said the night nurse's voice, "Mrs. Dinah's just had a seizure. We don't know if she'll make it."

"I'll be right there," Maren said. She bolted back into the bedroom and grabbed the clothes she'd left on the cedar chest. "Mom," she explained to Cleve, who was propped up on one elbow. "A seizure."

"You okay to drive?"

"Yeah, sure." Something was pounding in her ears. "I've got to rush. I'll call you."

The phone rang again as she scooped her keys off the buffet. "Mrs. Gledhill," the night nurse said, "I'm sorry. She's gone."

Cleve was standing next to her, "Should I go with you?"

"No," she sighed. "Come later."

The sun was just starting to lighten the eastern sky. She drove fast. There was no one else on the road. Why couldn't they have had some warning? Mom had been alone. Was she conscious? Maren hadn't thought to ask. They'd had a DNR on file. There were to be no ambulances taking Mom to the hospital. Maren had watched one of the other residents, Dorothy, her eyes full of terror, be gurneyed away, and she died then in the hospital instead of her own familiar room, cared for by people who knew her.

One of the aides unfastened the front door lock to let Maren in. She passed the night nurse in the hall. "Was she awake?" Maren asked. "Was she aware?"

"I don't think so," the night nurse said.

Was the nurse just trying to be kind? Maren didn't know the night nurse well the way she did the day nurses. She pressed close to Mom's bed. Mom was lying on her back, her eyes closed. Would the nurse have closed them? Mom was so still. Maren sank into the chair beside the bed and rested her head on the side bars.

That was one of the problems when Mom was living in her own home. No side bars on the bed. She'd somehow slide out of the bed onto the floor, and the care woman, usually Leticia, would have to get her up, which was hard because Mom had got heavy and she didn't cooperate. "Carrie pushed me out of bed," she would tell Maren when she got there. "I don't know why they don't believe me."

Even in the nursing home, when she'd get bruises on the thin skin on her arms, she would show them off to Maren. "Carrie pinched me," she would say, and Maren finally learned to say, "I wish Aunt Carrie wouldn't do that."

A sheet covered Mom's legs. They kept the nursing home warm enough so sheets were enough for most of the ladies, but Mom, who was extra cold, usually had a quilt or a soft afghan at night too. Not the special quilts or afghans that Grandma had made—those were back in Maren's own house, and she planned on giving them to her kids in a few years. These were machine-made quilts and afghans that the nursing home stocked in their cupboards. Maren lifted the sheet, then laid it back over her mother's legs. She had nice legs even though her body was thick. *This is the woman that my father adored,* Maren thought. She remembered his singing to the bathroom mirror when he was shaving, "Dinah, is there anyone fine—ah?"

Mom, Mom, Maren repeated in her mind. Are you where they say you are? With Dad and your folks and your sisters?

"What great rejoicing there must be in heaven," her cousin Jill said, when Aunt Ruth Ann died. Maren wasn't so sure. Dad hadn't believed that, and Cleve didn't. But it was a comfort if you could believe it. Unless Carrie was up there still pinching people.

The nurse came in to tell her that the funeral home would send their van about eight o'clock. They'd prepare the body, drive it all the way to Logan to the mortuary there. They'd have a graveside service, and Dad's ashes, stored all these years in a terra cotta box next to the fireplace tools, would go into the vault with Mom's coffin. "Together again," the obits like to say. The three sisters together too—at least in the same cemetery. And their parents.

And maybe someday her too. She and Cleve needed to talk about that stuff. And do wills, make plans. Make life easier for each other and the kids. It was their turn next, after all. She shivered a little. It wasn't anything she liked to think about.

Cleve's hands were on her shoulders. Nobody else's hands felt like that. *I'm a motherless child*, she thought, but somehow the weight of his hands lifted her up.

"I called the kids," he said.

She touched her mother's fingers. "Maybe I should take her ring," she told him. "Maddy lost hers, remember. Maybe she'd like her grandma's."

"You have your grandma's," Cleve said.

Maren looked down at the fat gold band on her own left hand. When she and Cleve had told Mom and Dad that they wanted to get married, Mom hadn't said anything at first. Then she had gone into her bedroom and come out with the ring. "I saved it for you," she had said. "Do you want it?"

Maren put her arm around Cleve's waist, the way she had done then, forty-one years ago. She looked up at him and held on. "I do," she had said then. And now again she said, "I do."

Elaine

Immersions

I.

CLINGING TO HER FATHER'S SLIPPERY BACK, ELAINE RODE
the cold waves. It was thrilling, but terrifying, and she squeezed
her hands around his throat until he said, in between breaths,
"Don't choke me, daughter. Relax."

It was not possible to relax. He breathed over his right shoulder and tipped her towards the left. Her turn would last just a few
minutes longer. They always did two laps around the wooden
raft where the people who knew how to swim sat and sunned
before splashing into the lake again. Now they were heading
towards the shore where Mama stood, the sun behind her so
her face was shadowed and where Ben and Stevie squealed and
jumped in the shallow water and waited for their rides. Even
though they were younger, they never seemed to slide off Daddy's back or squeeze his neck too hard. Stevie couldn't even do
the dead man's float, but he wasn't afraid.

Elaine shivered until Mama draped the blue sailboat towel
around her. "Don't go far," Mama said. "Practice your Articles
of Faith."

Elaine headed back towards the picnic tables. She already
knew her Articles of Faith—as long as she could get started and
keep the momentum going. She was pretty good at memoriz-
ing poems and though the Articles of Faith didn't rhyme, they
had a kind of beat and sound to them. She especially liked the
fourth one, the one with the "s" and "sh" sounds, "Baptism by
immersion for the remission of sins." She hung the towel from

the side of the table, found her glasses in their tan plastic case, then crawled under the bench into the shade. Tomorrow she would have to say any Article of Faith the Bishop asked. That was to prove she knew enough to be a member of the church. Last Saturday was her eighth birthday. Next Saturday she and Katie Toppler were going to be baptized in the special font in Las Vegas. Elaine slid onto her stomach, unrolled her comic book, and started to read.

II.

"NOW BEHAVE," MAMA SAID AS ELAINE AND BEN TUSSLED in the back seat of the Topplers' car. Katie was sitting primly behind Mrs. Toppler, who was driving, and Mama twisted around from the other front seat, where she usually sat in their own car. "She poked me," Ben said. "Elaine!" Mama scowled at her. "And on the day you're getting baptized."

It was *after* the baptism she would have to be good, but Elaine let go of Ben's wrist and squinted out the window at the sand and broken beer bottles. Mama had hoped Grandpa could come from Utah to baptize and confirm her, but Grandma wasn't well enough to make the trip, so old Brother Beck was going to fill in. Katie's father wasn't a member either, so Brother Beck had a double assignment. Elaine didn't like Katie very much. Katie wouldn't play with Rita because Rita was Catholic and her mother had run off somewhere and her father was dark and shrunken and had an accent. Elaine thought Rita and her father had funny things hanging on their walls, but she liked playing with Rita in their backyards. Their backyards were separated by the back alley. Yesterday Rita said she had been baptized when she was a baby.

In the dressing room, Mama smoothed down Elaine's white blouse and fastened a safety pin to cinch in the waist of the white cotton skirt. The skirt belonged to Jewel Farnsworth, the oldest daughter of the only other Mormon family on the block. The Farnsworths had three girls coming up after Jewel so a white skirt was a useful investment for them. Elaine's hair was in tight French braids, bound by white ribbons. Mama said braids made her look like a fence post, but no one would be taking pictures during the baptism anyway. She marched Elaine out to the edge of the font. Brother Beck was already there, wearing a white shirt and white pants and white belt but no shoes and socks. Of course she didn't have on shoes and socks either, but the idea of old Brother Beck barefooted struck her as enormously funny, and she had to swallow to keep from snickering.

"Just hold your breath," Brother Beck said, "when I say the words 'Holy Ghost.' You can lean back on my arm a little." When it came time, she closed her eyes, held her breath, felt herself guided into the water. She was scared. She stood up fast without waiting for Brother Beck to help. "Her pigtail stuck out," said a man standing at the side. Brother Beck didn't seem surprised. "We'll go deeper this time," he said. He took her hand and began again. "I baptize you in the name of the Father, and of the Son and of the Holy Ghost." This time he pushed her down. She struggled to rise and came up spluttering. "Okay," said the man on the side of the font. "She was all the way under."

Mama toweled her off a little as she waited for Katie, who had short hair and made it on the first try. Someone put up two folding chairs by the side of the font, and she and Katie sat down, each wrapped in a white towel. Brother Beck put his hands on Elaine's head first. Drops were still running down her forehead. Brother Beck had a little palsy and she felt his hands shake. Fascinated, she forgot to listen to the blessing. Suddenly everything seemed funny, and she had to strangle the laughs coming up from her stomach. She was shaking now more than Brother Beck. That seemed even funnier, and her cheeks ballooned and tears leaked out of her eyes. Then it was over and the reality of her mother's presence struck her and she sat up straight and willed the convulsions to stop. "I was choking on some water," she said. Mama eyed her strangely. "I'm okay now."

Later she wondered if she'd invalidated the baptism. If not the baptism, at least the confirmation. She couldn't possibly have received the Holy Ghost. It wouldn't have come to someone who wasn't paying attention and, even worse, who was laughing. Besides, she didn't feel any different than she did before.

III.

SHE WAS THE ONLY TEN-YEAR-OLD IN THE FROG CLASS. IT was humiliating. In the summer, every Tuesday and Thursday afternoon, she had to walk with Ben and Stevie to the school parking lot where the big yellow bus was waiting to take them to the lake. Everyone carried a towel and Jeffrey Johnson always snapped his at Elaine as she walked down the aisle to the back where her friends from school sat. As soon as the bus motor rumbled, someone would start singing "A hundred bottles of beer on the wall," but Elaine didn't pay much attention. She was worrying about the lessons. Tadpoles were just learning to float; Frogs were learning to do the breast stroke and the crawl; Class I's had mastered the front crawl and were learning the back crawl; Class II's could actually swim and were learning to dive off the raft. All Elaine's friends were Class I's except Gayle and Rita who were Class II's. This was the second year Elaine would be a Frog. She had learned to float quickly, but she could not propel herself through the water and take breaths of air at the same time. Even Stevie was a Frog this summer. Ben was already a Class I.

The bus tires sounded gritty at the end of the asphalt. The kids stampeded over the hot sand and into the cold water. Elaine hesitated only a minute. Today she would swim to the raft. She could do anything she set her mind on doing. She would wave at her teacher and then swim back. Then he would graduate her immediately into Class I.

Right arm, left arm, right arm, left arm. It was okay as long as her feet were touching bottom. When she felt the bottom fall away, she stroked once, twice, but nothing happened. She couldn't get her legs up. She started to sink. She batted her arms wildly and gasped, "Help!" but the water rushed into her mouth and she couldn't even hear herself. Flailing frantically with both arms, she finally twisted around to face the beach. She felt one foot touch sand. She stepped heavily back into the shallower water and looked about. No one was looking at her. No one could hear her heart pounding. No one had even noticed that she had almost drowned.

"I can't go swimming," she said to Mama the next Tuesday. "I have an earache."

Mama looked concerned. "Stay in, then," she said. "But no reading under the cooler. Sit on the couch."

The earache lasted the rest of the summer. It disappeared as soon as Ben and Stevie came home from the last lesson of the year. Stevie was now a Class I. Ben was a Class II. Elaine won a pen and pencil set in the library's Tom Sawyer contest. She'd read more books in three months than any other kid in town.

IV.

"I DON'T UNDERSTAND," SHE HEARD HER MOTHER SAYING to the doctor. One day she was well, reading movie magazines out in the back yard with Rita. They'd taken off their shoes and socks and were wriggling their toes in the sand and giggling about Eddie Fisher and James Dean. And the next day she was in the hospital with a temperature of 104. "Pneumonia is hard to understand," the doctor said. His voice echoed and he shimmered a little like the sand and broken glass alongside the road to Las Vegas. Then she was on a bed someplace between sleep and awareness. People were doing things to her body, prodding, pulling, patting, always gently. Suddenly she was enveloped in ice or ice water and the heat diffused and she slept.

V.

SHE WAS TIRED WHEN SHE STAGGERED OUT OF THE FRONT seat of Sister Pickering's stationwagon at the temple in St. George. They'd been on the road since five, and the twins, Joan and Jenny, had brought pillows and really seemed to be sleeping, but Burt and Mike were showing off for Katie and even though Elaine closed her eyes as if she were dozing, she heard their teasing voices bubble out of the back seat.

"Fourteen years old! I'll bet this is the first time you've been baptized for the dead," smiled the lady at the counter who gave her a heavy white jumpsuit that came down to her elbows and knees. "Two of you could fit in there," Mama would have said. Elaine peered out her dressing room door. Katie seemed to fill out her jumpsuit. Joan and Jenny had braided each other's hair. Elaine folded her arms in front of her body, but she felt exposed and foolish.

Someone opened the door and she saw the font. She was stunned, silent. From behind, Joan nudged her into a seat. It wasn't that the font was so big. She had imagined a rectangular pool, like the one she'd been baptized in, but bigger. But the temple font was a high sculptured tub that flattened the backs of a circled herd of enormous white animals. "Cows!" she breathed. "Those are oxen," Joan whispered impatiently. "Sit down."

Oxen. Had Sister Pickering explained this while her mind was wandering? Her mind wandered a lot, especially during church—but oxen? A man called Katie's name, and she stepped down into a circle of men in white. Elaine had left her glasses in the dressing room. She squinted to see better. After Katie was neatly, prettily dipped three times under three different names, she disappeared through the locker room doors. Next was Joan. Elaine looked over at Sister Pickering, who was smiling at the man at the podium. Elaine sat up, very straight, in her chair.

"You will be baptized for three people," said the man who called her name, "two women and a girl who died when she was about 16. First, Emily Ann Newark."

"I baptize you," said the man who held her wrist, "in the name of the Father, of the Son, and of the Holy Ghost." His brown eyes were the last things she remembered before she went under. Immediately she felt the terror. She thrashed upwards. "Her foot came out," said the man at the podium. "I baptize you," said the man with brown eyes, and this time she clenched shut her eyes and her hands.

"That was okay, but close," said the man at the podium. "Take her down deeper next time. Young lady, don't be so tense."

She nodded, but each time the water rushed over her, she stiffened. Then it was finished. Her arms again clutched in front of her, she found the dressing room. She dropped the soggy jumpsuit on the floor and rubbed herself with the towel. She couldn't get her face dry. Why I'm crying, she thought, surprised. She looked for her underwear, realized at once she hadn't brought a dry bra or underpants. She dressed without them, feeling oddly naked under her dress, then sat on the bench, very still, mewing softly as she exhaled. Someone knocked. She made herself take long breaths, blotted her face again, and opened the door.

"Are you all right?" Sister Pickering asked.

"I got water in my eyes," said Elaine. Sister Pickering motioned her into a room with a small table and a heavy, white-haired man. He nodded toward the chair in the center of the room and looked at the paper on the table. Elaine swallowed and sat. Her clothes felt rough against her body. Closing her eyes, she held onto the chair arms. There was heavy pressure on her head, but no tremor. She heard what was said, each of the three brief confirmations, but his voice seemed to come through gallons of water, muffled and dim.

VI.

PHIL ROWED WITH FIRM, DEFT STROKES, HIS SINEWY BACK already browning in the sun. Elaine pulled her new swimsuit's little skirt down over her bottom and leaned over the back of the dinghy. Last summer she wore the polka-dotted suit when she would lie out on a towel in the back yard or on the beach. She'd never got it wet. This spring the polka-dotted suit didn't fit quite right. She dangled her hand in the cold water. The lake was very deep here. They'd pushed Phil's brother's boat into the lake back past the swimming beach, and they must have come a mile already. Nick and Bev were sprawled in the front, facing Phil, their inner legs entwined, their outer hands each holding a bottle of beer.

"Way to go, Phil," Nick said. "You ought to get your Boy Scout rowing badge."

"I have it," Phil said. "*And* the canoeing badge."

"How about lifesaving?" asked Bev. "If one of us fell in, could you save us?'

Phil pulled the oars into the boat. "*And* the lifesaving badge. I'm going to be a lifeguard here when school's out. And maybe teach swimming." He raised an eyebrow at Elaine. "How about a Seven-up?" he asked, and she found a bottle in the cooler and handed it to him.

"Swim lessons are a big deal in Boulder City," Elaine said. "Twice a week, all summer, for all kids five and over."

"This where you learned to swim?" He raised the bottle towards his brother and reached over to take a bottle opener from Nick's hand. Phil and Nick's family had moved from Riverside in the fall.

"Kind of," Elaine said. "I wasn't one of the best students."

"As long as you can survive in the water." Phil took a gulp of Seven-up, wrinkling his nose as the fizz filled his nostrils.

"Boulder City keeps kids busy in the summer," Elaine said. "Some afternoons we did crafts over at the Veterans' building."

"I remember that," called out Bev, who was two years older. "We wove hot pads on little looms and made copper pictures."

"And Bible School," Elaine said. "You went to Bible School too, didn't you?"

"Sure," Bev said. "Everyone went to Bible School."

"Well, except the Catholic kids couldn't go," said Elaine. "But they wanted to. We sang 'Jonah Jonah Jonah Jonah, Jonah and the whale whale whale whale,' and made paper maché lemons."

"Sounds like good solid religious instruction," Phil said. He was all teeth and tan. Elaine had been thrilled Tuesday in Algebra when he asked her, "Would you like to go on my brother's boat Saturday?" He was the first exciting boy who'd asked her out. She'd only started going out last fall and the boys who took her places were boys from the next block, boys she roller skated with in grade school, not boys she dreamed of.

Yesterday she'd shaved her legs carefully and borrowed Rita's straw hat. This morning she'd fastened barrettes in her hair and put on her new prescription dark glasses. In a bag, she'd packed her brush and her mirror-case lipstick, baby oil, four tunafish sandwiches, and a sack of grapes.

She took off the straw hat and fanned her face. It was only May, but it was at least 90 degrees. She rummaged around in her bag for the baby oil. Suddenly the boat rocked. Phil stepped next to her, lifted her up, and thrust her over the side. She was suspended over the lake.

"No!" She writhed in his arms. "Don't!"

She beat against him, conscious of their laughter, more conscious of her own panic.

And then she felt the water, cold, merciless. She flailed and gasped. Phil was in the water beside her, holding her up. Her dark glasses were wet, but, a miracle, she was still wearing them and could see. Nick leaned over the side of the boat, Phil pushed her from behind. She reached up her arms, and Nick hauled her in. She scraped the fronts of both thighs on the rough wood, but she was out of the water, seated on the rower's bench, and Bev was blotting her dry with a towel. "Poor baby," Bev said. "That was mean."

Elaine tried to smile, but she was shivering too hard. Being a good sport, she thought, that was what was important. "That's the fastest way to cool off, I guess," she managed to say.

Phil looked sheepish. He sat down beside her and put his arm around her. "I couldn't resist," he said. "You looked so," he paused, "dry."

She shivered for a few more minutes, then relaxed. They all took their places, Elaine again in the back of the boat. Bev smeared a little zinc oxide on Nick's nose. Elaine brushed her wet straight hair. She felt limp, ugly. Phil started rowing again, slowly, moving the boat someplace even further from the shore.

VII.

THE EVENING RITA'S FATHER TOOK THEM TO DINNER AT the Golden Nugget, Elaine learned how to swim. She learned without even touching the water. They had eaten chicken in a fancy almond sauce and the waiter had brought them a little lavender cake with fifteen candles for Rita to blow out, and afterwards they strolled by the pool, the three of them, and Elaine was dazzled by the soft blue light under the water. In the pool were two women, and they stroked lazily, easily, one on her back, the other on her side.

What Elaine wanted to do was to slide out of the yellow flowered dress Mama had made her for Easter, and slip into the pool. She wanted to stretch out in the water and raise her right arm and bring it back high over her head and pull smoothly down. She understood immediately she had been doing everything wrong. She had been fighting the water instead of parting it with clean long strokes.

But now she knew. Tonight she would glide through her dreams like a dolphin. Tomorrow she would swim like a seal.

Long Divisions

IT IS ALIVE, THE COLORADO, ITS HEAVY BROWN WATERS pulsing through limestone and sandstone layers gouged out before it learned manners from the government and the Glen Canyon dam.

"She don't give a hot sheep shit," sings Terrill, oaring to his own beat. "She don't give a red-hot damn."

I smile into the sun, my scabbed, bandaged fingers warm on the hot, gray rubber. I am, without much hope, watching the river's edge for beavers. Across from me Rob is sunbathing on the raft's side. Sunbathing, that is, in a plastic yellow rainsuit and regulation orange life jacket, Coast Guard and Park Service approved. We're in between rapids, in between storms, in between the two main trails that connect the rims to the river. "I'm going to close my eyes," Rob says, "so I won't see any hikers."

"Why?" I ask. "They're closer to nature than we are." *We* got to the bottom of the canyon on the Navajo bus.

Only one person on our raft has been burning many calories today. I look over my shoulder at Terrill, our raftsman. He rotates his shoulders, his oars slack for the moment in their locks. He is perched on a muddy food locker. The other three boatmen and the boatwoman, Karly, keep their rafts and their locker seats clean, growl at us if we track in mud. Terrill tracks in his own mud. "Muscles sore?" I ask.

"Know anything about massage?" He looks at me through half-closed eyes. It's part of his act, these signals he sends. No woman wearing a wetsuit top, a wool shirt, a blue rain slicker, and a life jacket could look very desirable.

"How long before you get used to it?"

He shrugs. "Soon as I find me a ripe young woman."

"Maybe you need a rotten old chiropractor."

"I think I'll buy me an eighteen-year-old Somalian," he says, smiling into the river beyond me. He has already shed his life jacket—a yellow kayaker's number—and his rain slicker, and now he peels off his T-shirt, also yellow, faded, with M*A*S*H printed on the front in large letters. Behind him in the back of the raft, Lona, a laid-off schoolteacher from South San Francisco, and Mark, an accountant from Denver, both bundled like us in rain gear and life jackets, are gazing at the Redwall. Lona, I suspect, is trying to spot the first blue heron. Yesterday she was on Andy's boat with us, and she was the first to see the black-necked stilts. Like me, she is thirtyish and intense; unlike me, she is brave enough to spend a thousand dollars for a raft trip without knowing where next month's rent is coming from. She is outfitted with binoculars and nose plugs, the one to better see the heron with, the other in case we flip or she is bounced off the raft. In rough water, she clips on the nose plugs, and the binoculars swing heavily from her neck. In calm water, like now, she occasionally offers the binoculars to Mark. Mark is bland and smooth-chinned, apparently the only person in the canyon with a razor. Lona doesn't seem much interested in his company. I commend her judgment.

I turn sideways so I can see the ribboned wall of the gorge and squint up at Terrill at the same time. "Where do you call home then? Flagstaff?"

He waits a second before answering. "Yeah. Big Flag."

"You're not there much though."

"Enough."

"Live alone?" Rob stirs. Last night he told me that I asked Andy, yesterday's raftsman, inappropriately personal questions.

"Naw," Terrill says. "Got a lady or two to keep my bed warm."

"Or two?" I ask.

"But she don't give a piss ant's pus," he sings, oaring again in rhythm. "She don't give the Hooo-oover Dam."

The sky is too blue. Until yesterday we were wet from the rain as well as the river, and the contrast is startling. "I grew up by the Hoover Dam," I say and check to measure interest. None evident. "Close to Las Vegas." Terrill winces. "It's not what everyone thinks," I say. "The strip, the lights—that's all a stage front. Las Vegas is really just a big Mormon town. Poplar stands. Wide, straight streets. Rodeos. Church bazaars."

"Thought you two were from the Big Wormy Apple."

"We are now." I nod towards Rob. "He grew up in Salt Lake City."

"Another big Mormon town."

"Yeah."

"You big Mormons?"

Rob's leg jerks just a little. "Used to be," I say.

Terrill reaches for his life jacket. "Better wake 'im up. We're coming to Horn."

Rob opens his eyes, swings his legs down, gives me a brief look that I'm not up to interpreting, and assumes his ready-for-the-rapids pose; he clutches the blue ropes and stuffs his rubber-booted feet under the storage bags. I draw my rain hood over my billed hat and brace myself. Terrill is standing, assessing the brown foam. Karly's boat, just before us, drops suddenly, rises, is buffeted, rocks, and is calm. I look back to see Terrill, lips parted, lower himself to the food locker. Lona has donned her nose plugs. The boat rolls.

"Baby!" bleats Terrill, and we crash into a plume of water. "Didja see that hole? Wahoo!"

I loosen my hold a little and let myself feel the rises and falls. I hear Terrill's grunts and the oars grating in their locks and am conscious of walls of water washing in from over the side and front. Trying not to blink, I look straight ahead, and I swell again, inside.

"Bail!" yells Terrill. "Bail, you mothers!" The raft is still rolling hard. Rob manages to unlatch the buckets and hands me the small bailer, one fashioned from a plastic Purex jug. I realize I am sitting in water up to my waist. Furiously we scoop water up and over the sides. Terrill, breathing a little harder, slows his oars as the waves calm, shakes his head, his blond hair and beard wet and kinky. "Wahoo," he says again. "Whatta hole." He is examining his nails. "You drop in that hole and you've got a fifty-fifty chance." Mesmerized, I am holding the Purex jug motionless. "Keep bailing," he says, glancing at me briefly and tearing off a hangnail with his teeth. "We missed the hole by a good four inches."

The skeptic in me wonders if all of this hoopla is concocted for our entertainment. The pragmatist in me tells me just to enjoy it.

"Granite next."

"Sounds like the cross-town bus driver," Rob mumbles to me. He wipes off his sunglasses with the underside of his rain jacket. I scowl at him and tighten the drawstring on my hood.

"You ever worry?" I say back over my shoulder to Terrill.

"Sure," he says. He is stroking slowly, alternating oars. "About what?"

"The rapids. Flipping."

He shrugs. "There's a lotta things to worry about in this world. Like getting old. I worry a lot about getting old. Hey," he says, "next year I'll be thirty." He is silent, then refocuses on my question. "River's tricky. Complicated. Gotta know her." He runs his eyes down me again. "Like a woman."

Lona leans forward. Her voice twangs because of the nose plugs. "What's the worst river you've ever been on?"

Terrill listens for a moment to the rapids. "The worst? The worst is Puddle Creek, Nebraska. That's where I'm from. Puddle Creek, Nebraska." He stands again, and once more we follow Karly's boat into the roar and spray.

It is the best of days. Three big rapids, close on. In the third, we rise out of the water, nose almost straight up. We take the right run. Ahead of us Karly is following Andy and Buzz and Bags down the left. Water is pouring out of the raft faster than we can bail it, rushing out over the sides.

"Jesus Christ!" hollers Terrill. "You waiting for the resurrection? Bail, mothers, bail!"

Afterwards, gliding on smoother water, my eyes taking in the Muav and Redwall, I think, surprised, how a part of me shuddered when Terrill shouted "Jesus Christ." "Thou shalt not," said the yarn-framed poster on my bedroom wall, "take the name of the Lord thy God in vain." A second small poster, hung for symmetry maybe as well as for my spiritual welfare, began, "We believe in God, the Eternal Father, and in His Son, Jesus Christ, and in the Holy Ghost."

We've separated ourselves from that now, Rob and I. That's one reason we've stayed in the East, to ease that separation from our religious roots. It's been easier for me anyway than for him. Mom is a believer, Dad a non-believer, and I wobbled in the middle until I was twenty-two and took a faith-demoting pilgrimage to Israel. But Rob had clean hands, a pure heart, and a family that absolutely panted together in prayer. His faith began wavering at seventeen when he decided the world was about five hundred million years older than his Sunday School teacher, one Brother Emery, said it was. "Book learning," Brother Emery had snarled. "Book learning!"

Rob never could cut the cord clean though. He still has occasional recurrences of hope, like last June when his oldest sister, LaNell, got stomach cancer and the family begged us to join them one day in fasting and prayer. Rob wouldn't call it fasting, but he didn't eat for most of the week. At the end of the summer we flew back to Salt Lake for LaNell's funeral.

It's April now, time of rebirth, not death, and Terrill has taken off his life jacket again, and Rob has shed the pants of his yellow suit and is stretched out once more, navel down on the rim, facing the multi-colored canyon wall. The Hermit shale is frosted with pale sage-like brush. Terrill doesn't know its name, but it will be brown in a week or two he says. "A western tanager!" Lona calls out, and we all crane our necks to see and don't.

Terrill is swigging river water from the tin cup that he eats all his meals from. He gargles, then spits neatly over the oarlock into the river. He tosses me a plastic bottle of viscous white liquid and offers his back. I have to stand and lean to reach him. Over his right shoulder blade is a tattoo, two wild blue horses. I smear lotion on the wild horses, on his already red and freckled shoulders, down the curve of his spine. My rough hands and torn bandages grate against his skin.

"Doesn't this hurt?" I ask. "It's like getting a massage with sandpaper."

He grunts something to convey pleasure. Just above the waist of his cut-offs is a wide, curving line. "What's the scar from?' I hand back the capped bottle, noting that Rob is lying much too still to be asleep.

"Hippo," he says, shifting on the seat now washed clean by all the rapids, and picking up the oars. "On the Omo. Blind old mother hippo left her paw print on me. She thought my little gray raft was seducing her baby." He whinnies, rumbles, sways from side to side. "I was seducing a woman, for God's sake! Another guy's woman, matter of fact. Guy who hired me." He sets down the oars again. "Sheila. Sheila was all right. She was really ripe." He picks at a blister on his hand, holds it out to me. "See that? It's because it's the first trip of the season. By June there won't be no blisters." I return his hand, and he easily takes up the oars. "She kept coming to my tent," he says. "Her old man was pissed off but wasn't much I could do. Besides, he knew I was his best boatman." His eyes are on the river. "I'm the best boatman on five continents." He looks at me. "How many continents are there?"

"Seven, I think."

"Well. I'm only the best boatman on five."

"He's full of crap," Rob will say tonight as we zip ourselves into our separate mummy bags, the zippers, among other things, incompatible. But I believe Terrill's tale. I look straight ahead now, nodding into the river.

"I KEEP HAVING THESE FANTASIES," I TELL MARIE, A DEN-tal technician who is sitting beside me trying to pull off her rubber boots. "Fantasies of hot showers and chocolate ice cream." Beside us Rob is anchoring our ground cloth with enormous stones. I don't tell Marie of my other fantasies.

"Yeah," she says. "I keep dreaming about my waterbed. And you know what I'd really like? I'd really like to vacuum out my sleeping bag." She grits her teeth and grunts. "But it wouldn't do any good."

"There's a lotta upkeep to life." I've just yanked off the second of my own boots and am examining between my toes. Fungus can grow on wet feet, Paula has told us. Paula is a retired school nurse from Tucson who wears a pioneer bonnet and face powder to keep off the sun. She has medicine for foot fungus. Also for motion sickness, diarrhea, and yeast infections.

Terrill saunters past in his sneakers and cut-offs, the tan pockets flapping below the fringe. He pretends to ignore us, but our eyes catch for a second. Maybe he is really watching Marie, who is down to running shorts and a tank top. Marie is short, fair, twenty-one and overweight, but still quite pleasant looking. Last night she told me she prefers to date gay men. "Less suffering," she said. "But you probably can't remember how painful it is to be alone."

Terrill is wearing a small pack. He doesn't have dinner duty tonight, I calculate. He probably wants to get away from the rest of us. He'll camp off up the canyon. The sneakers mean serious business. Usually he hikes in sandals.

"I can't figure that guy out," Marie says. "Sometimes he acts like we're human beings, and sometimes he acts like we're toads."

She slides onto a broad, hot rock. "Elaine?" Her eyes are closed. "How'd you meet Rob?"

"In New York," I say absently. Something about Terrill's back lets me know he wants to be watched.

"How?"

Terrill disappears behind an outcrop. "I was coming back from Israel," I say. "I was staying with a friend from college. She knew him." I struggle out of my plastic pants and peel off my wet wool ones. "It's like they're the seniors," I tell Marie, "and we're the freshmen."

"Who?"

"The boatmen."

"Yeah," she says. "The lowly freshmen. Except Buzz. He doesn't act like that. And maybe Bags." She yawns. "What were you doing in Israel? Did you know Terrill was in Israel a couple of years ago?"

I turn my rubber booties inside out to dry. "How do you know?"

"Buzz told us yesterday. He was a spy or a security guard or something." She runs her finger over her chapped lips. "If you can believe anything Terrill tells anybody."

I drape my wool and my plastic pants over a stiff-limbed bush and pull on my shorts. "I lived on the biggest kibbutz in Israel," I say, propping my back against the base of Marie's rock. "It was kind of like here. None of us knew anything. Foreign kids on a farm vacation. Six months to pick olives and grapefruit and learn a little Hebrew." I pour lotion onto my hands and scrape them together. "We didn't know how to survive on a farm. And the Israeli kids could've treated us like yokels, the way the boatmen treat us, but they didn't. The boatmen figure they *could* be like us if they wanted—you know, going to school and having regular jobs and regular salaries—but that's too tame and boring for them. They can *afford* to look down their noses at us."

Rob slides onto the sand beside me, lays his head on my hip. "You've put her to sleep," he says, nodding his head backwards. Marie is breathing deeply. She starts to make small snoring sounds. "Keep talking," Rob says. "I need a nap too."

I keep talking. "The Israelis really *were* superior to us. At least in everything that counted over there. They were big and healthy, and they knew how to run tractors and shoot guns. They'd been over every inch of Israel almost, in the army." I think of my Israeli boyfriend, Igal, who had just finished his military service when I arrived at the kibbutz. He was big and healthy. And beardless. I feel Rob's mustache. It is getting scraggly, and his chin and cheeks are covered with black bristle. The boatmen all started with scraggly mustaches and wild, prophetic-looking beards. I remember what I was saying. "But we foreigners seemed exotic, special to them. They *couldn't* be what we were, even if they wanted that. They didn't have the money to go to America or England or Belgium or Holland. They'd never been to college."

"Don't feel guilty," Rob says. "They probably sat around in their cabins talking about what turkeys you all were."

I knot the bandanna at the nape of my neck. I lost my faith in Israel. It didn't survive my separation from Mormon culture and my visit to Yad Vashem and the life-size photographs of the holocaust. Rob's head becomes heavier as he relaxes. I lie still, feeling like the only person in the world who is awake. I could reach over and get my *Guide to Wild Life in the Canyon*, but I've already read the beaver chapter six times.

Karly is skimming barefoot over the rocks. Walking on these rocks is as miraculous to me as walking on water. I wonder about her relationship with the men who oar these rafts. Especially Terrill. Karly is pretty. She has thick braids, black except for a shock of white at one temple. She was in New York, secretary for an ad agency, she told us, the day we were on her boat. She hated it. Cousin talked her into going to whitewater school with him, and presto! her life changed. In her former life, she worked three blocks over and one down from where I work. I write letters all day too, though I don't type them. I compose them into a Dicta-phone, obsequious letters to appease disgruntled customers.

I envy Karly's style. Even in my Sierra Sneakers, I have trou-ble hiking down the talus. On yesterday's hike I skidded on a rock, crashed onto my left hand, and slashed off the tip of my third finger. I am, as always, without grace.

I look up at the cliffs. Kaibab limestone, Toroweap, Coconino sandstone, Hermit shale. They quiz us on it continually, the boatmen, Karly. "All right! Who can spot the Muav limestone?" All heads swivel. "See the Great Unconformity? An extra chop at dinner for anyone who can figure out what fossils we'll find in the Bright Angel." I try rhythmic mnemonic patterns. Kaibab, Coconino, Hermit shale. Supai, Redwall, bail, bail, bail.

"See up there?" On yesterday's hike Terrill had pointed to the rim of the canyon, only then I didn't know he had wild blue horses tattooed on his shoulder blade. "The Kaibab and the Toroweap alone are more than five hundred feet thick. And that's just the frosting." He had just salved my damaged finger and was holding my left hand up, pressing it to slow the bleed-ing. The cap of the finger was attached by a small sliver of flesh. I was too surprised to hurt. "And people," he said oblivious of the blood running down both our arms, "people are about an inch of the top layer. Maybe not even an inch."

He pressed a bandage hard on the top of the finger and held it a minute. We were silent. I was thinking about bleeding on Ter-rill and holding up the hike. Rob was probably thinking about the age of the earth, the Precambrian and Paleozoic divisions. I don't know what Terrill was thinking.

We've seen traces of life millions of years older than man. I wonder how Rob's old Sunday School teacher would explain all this. It's more than book learning. Rob is still dozing on my hip. I don't wake him to ask.

One afternoon we felt with our roughened fingers the smooth impressions of nautiloids in the limestone. The number of years dazzles me for a few minutes—then fades into the abstractions to which I relegate all numbers over thirty-two. Besides, I say to myself, I'd rather see a beaver. Yet another recurring fantasy. Young kids who grow up in the desert and old kids who grow middle-aged in the biggest of cities are zoologically deprived. Sometimes on the river we pass what Bags tells us are beaver holes, but none of us, this trip, have yet seen the real thing. I'm not sure I even believe in the real thing. Easter bunnies. Easter beavers. Hobbits and griffins. Mock turtles.

Rob and Marie are still asleep. I hear pots banging. Karly and Bags have dinner detail. I slide out from under Rob's head. He stirs and opens his eyes. "I think I'll go help with supper," I say.

"You don't have to. We paid for this trip."

"I don't like being waited on. They're doing all the work."

"I don't know." He raises himself up on one elbow and looks at me. "Sometimes it's hard work just hanging on."

IN THE MORNING WHILE BAGS IS FLIPPING EGGS OVER THE porta-stove, Terrill, fresh from his overnight outside the camp, slides behind him, catches an egg in his tin cup, and disappears behind the cliffside. Bags is thick-necked, short, hairy, and docile. I suspect he doesn't remember anyone's name. "Can we ride with you today?" I ask.

"You bet, dear," he says. "We do Crystal first thing." He winks. "Last time I did Crystal, I flipped." He winks again, and I don't know whether he is serious or not. I take a swallow of my oatmeal. I decide to believe him. I have decided, haven't I, to believe them all?

"Hey," says Paula, already decked out in her pioneer bonnet. "Know what today is?"

"Sunday," says Mark. He looks at his waterproof, shockproof, digital wristpiece that adds, subtracts, multiplies, divides up to six places, calculates square roots, and plays "Oh, Susannah." It also, he has shown us, tells four time zones, converts to a stopwatch, and indicates AM and PM in case the wearer can't tell the difference.

"*Easter* Sunday," says Paula, and she sticks her plate of fried eggs in front of Bags's face. "I'd like mine with a chocolate bunny."

"Easter," repeats Mark.

"Well!" says Terrill, reappearing in back of Bags. "Hot sheep shit. Easter."

Bags is quiet on the boat. He rolls his whole body forward when he oars. He has brought us through Crystal without mishap, without event either—almost mechanically. We turn to see, two boats back, Terrill's raft rolling through the rocks, Terrill seeming to stand atop a wave.

Rob is talkative today. He asks Bags if he prefers skiing in Montana—Bags come from Bozeman—or Arizona. Is it harder to find temporary work in the winter or the summer? Does Bags think they should relocate the burros or shoot them? Rob loves either-or questions. His idea of a showstopper is to ask a preschooler in the company of his parents whom he prefers—his mommy or his daddy. We are bumping through the jewel-named rapids. The names seem incongruous. "Why not Toilet Bowl?" I say. "Or Spin Cycle?" Bags looks over his shoulder and smiles patiently.

"Elaine's not a romantic," Rob explains.

Rob is, of course, wrong. I am right now dreaming as the rafts loll a little, drifting fairly close together. We're in the back of the raft today. I sit in the crook close to Bags's seat locker and look at where we've been. Behind us, Karly is oaring alternately, slowly, relaxed. Terrill seems to be picking at his knee.

In the front of our boat, Jerry P. is snapping pictures of the canyon, of us, of the other boats. He has a Tupperware container with twenty-five rolls of film in it. I like Jerry P. "What roll are you on?" I call.

"Seven."

"Long way to go."

"Might not make it through 'em all."

Jerry P. is the other transplanted westerner. He left Sacra-
mento after college to become a soil engineer in New Jersey. A
soul engineer, says Rob, who also likes Jerry P. We call him Jerry
P. to distinguish him from Jerry A., or Big Jerry. Jerry A. owns a
roofing company in Barstow. I've noticed he thinks he owns his
wife too, a large blond woman with no contrary opinions. All
of Jerry A.'s opinions are contrary. "It's good for us to be around
someone like him," I tell Rob. "A real redneck. Broadens our
horizons."

"You ever been back east?" I smile now at Bags.

"No, dear. Not yet."

"Want to go?"

"Maybe. When I'm real old."

"Like thirty?"

"Yeah." He leans over, scoops up a cup of brown river water
and drinks it. "Lots of places I want to go first."

"Like where?"

"Alaska. And Peru. Even Guatemala. Terrill sometimes does
winter runs in Peru and Guatemala." We pull into shore behind
Buzz's boat. "Lunch," says Bags.

We lumber off the rafts, dragging the wooden folding table
and the big bailing bucket, alias the hand-rinse barrel, to which
will be added some compound strong enough to disinfect a
whole hospital. I help peel and chop hard-boiled eggs. To cel-
ebrate Easter. Rob hates egg-salad sandwiches, I think, with a
touch of malicious pleasure. But there's always peanut butter for
the dissenters.

Buzz, the tallest and hairiest of the boatmen, Marie's favorite, is squatting on a rock with his harmonica. He plays a tune
I struggle to recognize, minorish and slow. I have a miserable
melodic memory. What words go to that? I fluff out the wad-
ded alfalfa sprouts. "Chow!" croons Andy. Rob and Jerry A. are
first in line. There is yellow bread and wheat. Egg bread, I think,

and then I remember what the tune is. "Hatikvah." One of those songs we were supposed to sing on the kibbutz but didn't very often. I have it on a record though. I can really only remember the last word, *Yerushaleim*—Jerusalem. I hum it with Buzz now.

"What's that matzoh music?" I hear Terrill's voice behind me; but when I turn, he is addressing Buzz. "Don't you know that Jesus Christ is your lord and savior?"

I forget I am still holding the egg-salad spatula. I have heard Terrill expound on Reagan and Rastafarians and the U.S. Marines and Friends of the Earth, a variety of convictions in a variety of voices, but this is a new lecture topic with a new intonation. Are we supposed to laugh?

Terrill leans into the circle he is making around Buzz, moving slowly, rhythmically. "It's true," he chants. Buzz straightens up, still blowing on the harmonica. Terrill waves his empty cup. "Here I was at the tomb in Jerusalem, and I was really feeling something for once when this puking priest comes up and asks for a donation. 'Look,' I told him, 'I'm having a religious experience for the first time in my life and you're asking for money?' He's sorry, he's sorry, the old guy says, and he backs off." Terrill bows and shuffles backwards, looking a little like a Chinese vaudeville performer. Those close by are watching, eyes amused over their egg-salad sandwiches. They know how to react. This is just another of his little solos. Karly smiles uncomfortably as if she has heard it all before. She lets out a little sigh. Buzz keeps playing what seems to me an appropriate accompaniment to the sermon.

"Jesus lives," says Terrill. "I maybe knew it in the back of my head all along, but then I really knew it." He closes his eyes for a second. "Jesus Christ is the savior of the world."

I stand all amazed. I have the impression that I am the only one who is really listening. Terrill maybe senses that because he looks at me for an instant, then makes another circle around Buzz. "Enough matzoh music," he says. "A hymn. An Easter hymn." Buzz lowers his harmonica for a second, nods, and lifts it again to his lips. He erupts into "When the Saints Go Marching In." A few, those who have finished their sandwiches and have free palms, start to clap. A few more sing. Terrill leads with gusto, waving his tin cup. "And when the new," clap clap clap clap, "world is revealed," clap clap clap clap.

"Don't forget to eat," Rob whispers into my hair. I look down at the immobile spatula and spread myself a sandwich. It tastes heavy, lumpy. I swallow it without really chewing and wash it down with pink lemonade. The song ends, but the clapping continues a few minutes until everyone scatters to clean up or suit up. Just before Andy and Bags fold the table, Terrill swipes a few gingersnaps and steps close to me to fill his cup with lemonade.

"You didn't get a sandwich," I say. I am struggling with the middle buckle of my life jacket.

He swallows his lemonade in one gulp and clips the cup onto a belt loop. "Some things are more important than food." He fastens my middle buckle for me. "Some things are even more important than sex," he says. "But not very many."

IN FEBRUARY, BACK IN OUR STUDIO ON EAST 96TH STREET, on top of the linoleum-topped slab that covers our bathtub and serves as our kitchen table, our friend Jean laid out all her snapshots. She had ridden the Colorado the summer before, with another outfitter, one that used dories instead of rafts. "Halfway through," she had told us, "I looked at myself in my steel mirror and said, 'What are you doing here?'" She had stacked up the snapshots while she talked and then dealt them out again like a pinochle hand. "But after a day the sun came up and my reservations disappeared." She spread out the pictures again. "I loved the rest of the trip," she said.

Because of Jean, I have prepared myself for letdowns, relapses. I have felt none. My knee slips out of joint scrambling up and down the trailless hills in Deer Creek Canyon. But ahead of us

Terrill is singing what seems to be "Amazing Grace" with a reggae beat, and I snap my rebellious knee back in. Up Havesu my bare legs are abraded by stinging nettle, and my camera, lodged with my canteen in a daypack, gets wet when I ford the creek. This time I don't have to fall; the creek reaches my armpits while I'm standing. "Oh well," Rob says, "the pictures of the bighorn wouldn't show up without a telephoto anyway." And Jerry P. offers to have copies made of the best of his twenty-five rolls of film.

I am on a day-after-day high. I am faintly conscious of the speed at which time is passing, but even that seems no reason for depression yet. Except for Mark and Buzz, we have no clocks and no calendars. We tell days by rapids. Everyone has been discussing the big one, Lava Falls, rated eight to ten in our plastic river books, legendary granddaddy of North American whitewater. Both Bags and Buzz flipped there last year. And Buzz had never flipped anywhere else.

Sitting in a lotus position on her sleeping bag, her binoculars at rest on her air pillow, Lona reckons that the safest place to be is with Andy. Andy, she says, has a perfect record. "No flips anywhere."

"Andy," says Jerry P., "has only been down this river four times."

"Odds are against anyone flipping twice in a row," says Mark. "I'm going with Bags."

Marie looks up from her can of diet Sprite. "Good reasoning," she says, "but I'll be on Buzz's boat. If I have to flip, I want to go with him."

"I'm going for the big ride," says Jerry P., shielding his camera from the late afternoon sun as he changes rolls of film. "I'm going with Terrill."

"Me too," I say. I glance at Rob. "Us too."

THE BOATMEN ARE VISIBLY TENSE ON LAVA MORNING, BUT that might just be for show, I think. If so, it works. Waiting, shifting about in the wet sand, stuffed into our rain suits and life jackets, we all feel tense. The mood melts a little when Terrill starts springing like a wallaby from boat to boat. I'm wishing I could collect his imitations. I have watched him do a dozen canyon wrens (he talks with them "like St. Francis," he says), a mama hippo, a baby hippo, two crazed lions (one in front of the Ethiopian safari van he was riding the roof of, the other through the wall of his and Sheila's collapsed tent), an angry father, Henry Kissinger (Matzoh Man), Jimmy Cliff, and about forty weeping, ranting, oversexed, undersexed, willing, or reluctant women. "Oh, Terrill," he raises his voice to a falsetto, "I have a head-ache." Or "Terrill, why can't you be a cattleman like my daddy?" or "You'll never amount to anything, you son of a bitch. You're wasting my best child-bearing years." Rob chastises me because I enjoy the performances so thoroughly, openly, uncritically.

Above Lava, we all pile out of the boats to assess the situation, the boatmen and Karly huddling on the rocks below us, calculating. When they finally return, Rob chews on his knuckle scabs and mutters in a tone I am familiar with, "Well, at least today God's on our side." I feel baked in my life jacket and rain suit. I hear Bags saying to Buzz, "Yeah, but there isn't a right run."

Andy goes first. Lona is sitting primly in the front, nose plugs firmly in place. The Jerry A.'s are hunched over in the back. The raft slides down left of center and rises clumsily, teetering, then rises, fast, and falls, hard, out of our view. We hear their squeals and see them bobbing and bailing further down. Buzz is ready, waiting.

Terrill has been chewing gum, but he spits it sharply into the river, then climbs onto our boat with the anchor rope in his teeth. "Matzoh's better than macho," Rob grumbles, but like Jerry P. and bonneted Paula in the back of the raft, like me across from him in the front, he nervously watches Terrill's face. Terrill fastens his life jacket slowly, looks at his blisters, oars out into the middle of the river. "One up," he says. "Four to go." Buzz's boat moves, again down the left. Terrill is standing. "Looks like he's going for that hole," he says calmly. "Looks like he's gonna hit it." The boat, we can see, is perpendicular, then flips back on itself. It is too low for us to see well. "One down," Terrill says. "Don't worry. I see Marie. Andy'll pick 'em all up."

I chew on my lip and watch Karly and Bags exchange grim looks. When the river is clear, Bags goes, again down the left, but not so far this time. We hold our breaths. "Cleared it," says Terrill after we see the thrashing. He makes a fist at Karly, who doesn't reply. She follows as exactly as she can in Bags's trail.

"Okay, guys," says Terrill, becoming more animated. "We're taking the right run!" I imitate Rob's hanging-on pose, stuff both boots under the storage bags, grip the blue front ropes, and crouch, head up to see what is coming. An enormous brown wave is coming. "Jesus Christ!" yells Terrill, and I wonder for the smallest of seconds if he is praying. I repeat to myself, "Jesus Christ." We catch the wave on the tip. The oars are shrieking in their sockets, and Terrill says again, softer, "Jesus!" I am filled with an odd joy. We climb another wave, plunge down it, into two hitting from the sides. For a minute I wonder if I'm in the boat or out of it. There is water everywhere. We are climbing again.

And then Terrill is bouncing on the locker seat, yipping to the other boatmen. I bail, feeling myself smile beyond all control. The rafts are quite close. Everyone is back in Buzz's now upturned boat. Rob waves at Marie who makes a small hand movement and shivers. Paula is leaning over the back side of the raft, wringing out her hat. Jerry P., his arm still slung through the handle of a bailing bucket, is struggling to undo his plastic camera case. I snap my bailer back on the ropes and grin up at Terrill. He half closes his eyes.

We glide downstream for a while, the winds not objecting, all feeling as if we've accomplished something, although most of us of course haven't. Still, Karly says karma determines if a boat can right itself. I don't know too much about karma. Maybe it's akin to the Holy Ghost.

"The motor rigs are always losing beer in Lava," says Terrill. "It floats down here. I've picked a lot of beer out of these waters." He smiles sleepily. "And some other things. Two oars. All I need now is my own boat." He hands me his tin cup, motions towards the river. I fill it and hand it back to him. "'Course the oars were different lengths." He hands back the cup for a refill. "Best thing though was an eighteen-year-old woman. Fell out of Karly's boat. 'Oh Terrill!'" His falsetto again. "'I'm so cold I'm gonna die. I think I've got hypothermia. Cure me! Cure me!'" He laughs and gulps the water in one swallow. "Yep. River's been good to me."

That afternoon we are all playful, elated. Around us the reds, buffs, grays, greens are dazzling. Here and there enormous rivers of lava surge down the canyon walls. When we finally pull the boats in, we toss high the heavy rubber duffels we've been dragging and pushing down the unloading lines for the past two weeks.

The boatmen and Karly gather on Bags's boat and sit in a circle drinking beer, swatting Buzz on the back and shoulders. They speak softly but urgently. Some of us unroll our sleeping bags on the sand in another sociable circle. We sit on them, pulling off wet boots and outer clothing, rubbing lotion on our hands and faces, opening cans of beer and pop. Jerry P. stretches out on his bag, his camera dormant for a minute at his side. Then he sits bolt upright. "Hot sheep shit," he begins, and we all guffaw. Then he says, "I don't want to go home."

"Me either," says Paula, snapping shut her powder case.

"Damn," says Jerry P. "I gotta be at work Tuesday morning."

"No work talk allowed," warns Marle.

There is no talk at all. Rob lies on his back looking at the too-blue sky. Jerry P. draws idly in the sand. I reach for my daypack, break through the tamarisks and brittle mesquite, and head for the cliffs. After a while, I hear Rob splintering branches behind me.

"Want to be alone?"

"In a minute. Hey." I look at my feet. A small animal skull is lying there. I pick it up and run my rough fingers along its smooth, perfectly formed teeth. "Good orthodontist." I hold it out to Rob. "I want to move back. We belong in the West. Even if it has to be California."

Rob makes a face. "Elaine, the only place I could get a transfer to is L.A. That's no different from New York. A big city's a big city."

"Some big cities are closer to what matters."

He scuffs his sneakers in the sand. "We can think about it," he says softly. "We'll have a better perspective when we're back home."

"I don't want a better perspective. You hope I'll forget about it. And New York's not our home."

He takes the little skull. After a few minutes he asks, "What do you think it was?"

"Alas, poor Yorick." I shrug.

"Not a beaver anyway. Not unless it wore braces."

I turn towards the cliff. He lays down the skull and slips back through the tamarisk. Finding my first foothold, I edge up the granite. It's always easier to climb up than down. I already know I'll be sorry. I keep on climbing. Maybe, I think, Rob will tell the boatmen about the skull, and maybe one of them will shoulder through the mesquite now, and maybe he'll find me, trapped on a ledge, unable to come down, unable to go up, and he'll rescue me on the back of a wild blue horse and carry me off to a hidden cave in the Bright Angel shale. But the boatmen are drinking on Bags's boat. At the end of a trip, the boatmen, too, will go back to work. They'll go back to Lee's Ferry and get back on the river.

Gingerly I make my way skyward. I perch on a rough rock, high enough to see the five boats lined up along the bank, too high to see who is sitting where. The ground cloths and bedrolls are tiny, insignificant splashes of color on the sand. The wind is getting fierce. I feel vulnerable up here. A few shrill sounds from the kitchen rocks carry up on gusts.

I lower myself down the rough, jagged slopes, mostly with my hands. My feet slide out from beneath me, and I catch myself with my palms on the schist. My right hand starts bleeding; my legs are scraped white. I move very slowly, out of sight of camp so no one can see my clumsy descent. I keep sucking my right hand so I won't leave a trail of blood. We are not, after all, supposed to litter in the canyon.

Finally, just as I am about to explode with impatience and fear, I reach the base of the cliffs. Someone else is there too, squatting, examining the little skull. I draw in my breath and hide my hand behind my back, pressing the palm hard with my fingers.

"Your old man told me you found something, dear," says Bags, straightening up. "Probably a ringtail cat."

With dinner, clam sauce on spaghetti, our spirits revive. The boatmen have put together a freeze-dried, gooey cheesecake, and we all take big portions and settle on the sand. I have bandaged my palm. Buzz gives instructions on the final half-day on the water. The Californians start planning a reunion in San Jose.

"We can come back next year," Rob says as we lie in our mummy bags and stare at the stars.

I have already thought of that. "I thought we were going to try to have a baby next year."

"Which do you want most?" I hear the playful tone of his either-or questions.

"I don't know what I want." I close my eyes on the star-speckled sky.

I sleep poorly. For the first time since we came into the canyon, I dream about the office. I rouse myself awake. Next to me I hear Rob's daytime breathing. I consciously slow down my breaths so I'll sound asleep and I roll over, towards the river.

THIS LAST MORNING WE ARE SUPPOSED TO FLOAT DOWN to Diamond Creek in silence. Rob has put our bags on Karly's raft, and we climb aboard in the gray dawn and shove off. It's too dark to see who is in what other boats, but everyone is quiet and anonymous anyway, and the distance between the rafts stretches out. Oars splash. I scour the shoreline for beaver holes. I look beyond the dark deep canyon walls at the whitening sky. The last stars have just disappeared. The bowels of the earth. We and the river have descended sixteen hundred million years.

This would be an appropriate time, I think, for a religious experience. I try to recite one of my childhood prayers. Heavenly Father. Bless Mommy and Daddy, Stevie and Ben, Grandmas and Grandpas. I concentrate hard. Grandmas and Grandpas, soldiers and sailors, beavers and wallabies. I hear irreverent noises behind us. Terrill, brushing his teeth and gargling. In the half light Karly frowns. Suddenly the canyon is full of small noises. A canyon wren. Terrill's whistled response. The bending and twanging back of a willow at the water's edge. I look closely through the gray; and though I don't see it, part of one of my prayers has been answered. I have heard a beaver.

And we are at Diamond Creek. We derig the rafts and scrub them out, splashing water on them and us with the bailing buckets. We load the boats on the waiting truck, load our gear on the waiting Navajo bus. Drenched, numb, we move awkwardly about on the sand. "Karly and Andy and I will be on the bus with you," says Buzz. "Bags and Terrill are riding with the boats back to the warehouse. Better tell 'em goodbye. Some of you got planes to catch in Phoenix."

We have a plane to catch in Phoenix. Alarm rises within me. Rob steps toward Terrill and thrusts out his hand. Another Mormon-town trait. Jerry P. is slapping Bags on the back. I hang back, confused, caught in the milling and lining up. I push behind Paula who is cuffing Terrill on the cheeks and stick out my hand in his direction. He looks at me with some amazement. "Holy Christ, woman," he says. "Don't you have no manners?" He hugs me roughly in his left arm, then turns abruptly to Marie who gives him a hard kiss. Marie has wet eyes. So does Jerry P. Bags squeezes my shoulders. "You're a good scout, dear," he says.

I stand helpless until Rob takes me by the elbow like an old lady and leads me onto the jammed and rickety bus. I am sitting on a rubber duffel in the aisle behind him. I am too far from the window, as we shift into gear and rumble up the gravel road, to see the canyon or the river or the truck. I stare instead at my hideous hands. The bandage on my palm is spongy with water. The one on my finger is fraying. I peel it slowly off. The finger is healed and, miracle of miracles, is smooth and pink, just the tiniest line showing where the top had lifted off.

"Hey," Karly is saying. She is wedged between me and Jerry P. and is examining his palm on her knee. "Look at that lifeline. You're going to live to be a hundred and twenty-five. She runs her finger down another crease. "This is your progeny line. Look out, New Jersey. Big Daddy is coming!"

"And this," Jerry P. points to a cracked knuckle, "is my water line." Karly laughs. Keeping his hand between her knees, she reaches for mine.

"Can't read you," she says, "unless you take off that bandage. What'd you do to yourself?"

"She was trying to slit her wrists," says Jerry P., leaning over. "These New Yorkers don't know nothing about anatomy."

"These New Jerseyans don't know nothing about grammar."

Behind us Buzz has extracted his harmonica from the pack I am sitting on. "Who wants a little matzoh music?" he says.

"Matzoh music! Let's have matzoh music!" calls out Marie. She slaps her thighs. But Buzz plays instead, in loud chords and heavy accents, "When the Saints Go Marching In," and everyone, even Rob, even I, clap with our wounded hands and sing.

Havesu

E WATCHES ELAINE'S BUTTOCKS, THE TAN SHORTS browned at the seat, as she walks briskly ahead of him on the narrow trail. Her dirty orange daypack bounces on her back, the leaky canteen a long wet lump on the right, the camera a squarish bulge on the left, separated by the other things she's stuffed in—toilet paper, hand lotion, capless ballpoint pens, little sticky rectangles of sugarless gum, and a ragged paperback so she'll never have to waste time. In honor of nature on this trip she's left behind Isaac Bashevis Singer and has limited herself to guidebooks on plant and animal life in the Grand Canyon.

When Rob first met her, six years ago now, at Jody's flat, she was smudged and sweaty after a twenty-hour charter flight from Tel Aviv, two jolting bus rides from Kennedy, and a four-story climb from 93rd Street proper. She dumped that same dirty orange pack upside down on Jody's mohair rug. "I've simplified my life," she said. "These are all my possessions." There were, he remembered, some travelers' checks, her passport, a Swiss army knife, some cotton underwear and T-shirts, all stamped with the Hebrew letter aleph by a kibbutz laundry, a camera with sand gritting somewhere in its innards, a poetry anthology dating from her undergraduate years at the University of Nevada, and a blue paperback copy of the Book of Mormon that she said she'd stopped reading but was holding onto for sentimental reasons. She'd given away a cheap guitar and the rest of her clothes. Finally, however, she admitted to owning boxes of books and a carton of aunt-embroidered dish towels and box-top-bought stainless steel spoons and forks—no knives—all of which arrived just before they were married.

The orange pack suddenly looms larger. He slows his step so he won't run into her; she hikes unevenly, racing for fifteen minutes, then dawdling for twenty. She holds a pronged ocotillo branch aside for him now. "Careful. I'm too poky for you."

"Poky." He pokes at her ribs and she sucks in her stomach. "Funny word, poky. Poke. I wonder what it means in cowpoke."

She shrugs. "You could still run on ahead, you know. You could probably catch the boatmen if you went now."

"I'll stick with you. Even if I won't get a Technicolor, wide-screen account of Terrill sleeping with the queen of Siam."

"He didn't sleep with the queen of Siam," she says. "Did he?"

"Elaine," he says. "Keep walking."

She speeds up both her step and her speech. "Look," she says, "you'll wish you'd gone when they get back and start talking about it. You'd get to see Moony Falls and maybe the reservation. You could take the camera. Get some pictures of the stone gods the Indians used to scare their children."

"The stones aren't the gods. The stones are the children. Bad children got turned into stone." With one hand he slaps at a bug trying to burrow through the stubble on his face; with the other he searches his pockets for the Cutter's. "I can carry the camera though."

"No. I want to carry it." She feels around her back with her left hand, pats the bump. She is talking over her right shoulder. "You'll have to work up gradually again to your daily ten miles. Hanging onto a raft and hiking a little won't do it. Especially eating like porkers. Maybe if you rowed. How many miles would you have to row to equal running ten?"

"I don't know." He spreads insect repellent on his hair for good measure, then shifts his attention to the creek. A river really, it spreads out, rolls over a flat layer of rocks, drops half a foot. They've come about a mile from where it spills into the

Colorado, from where they left the rafts tied up, one to another in the surprise inlet in the sheer limestone walls. "Why don't you get a picture?" he says.

She squirms out of the backpack, reaches in. Fiddling perfunctorily with the adjustments, she aims at the foam and snaps. She drops the camera again into the pack. She lost the lens cover a week after he'd given her the camera, a Christmas present to replace the series of sandy instamatics.

The canyon is green. Like spring in the canyons back home. Old home, that is, the Wasatch Range, the Uintas, where he used to go off by himself summer days—biking the old three-speed up two-lane highways with camp stove and sleeping bag weighing down the rear tire, or packing in with Eddie who always got nosebleeds at high altitudes. One time the creek flushed them out of a canyon on their homemade kayak. They wrecked on the rocks and crawled up the bank just in time. Borrowed truck bed empty, they drove, squeaking with mud and sobered with fear, back down to the valley. They didn't bang the back screen, but Mom wailed, "Don't sit on anything, don't even stand there, get straight under the shower," while LaNell and LouAnne, big sisters, always virtuous and clean, squealed their disgust. Mom and Dad and Eddie the Unmarried still hold down the purple brick house with the bent tree in front. LaNell and LouAnne long ago moved to their own brick houses. Only LaNell is dead now proving God knows what. If God knows. If God.

"Are you thinking about your long-lost youth?" Elaine shakes her hands as she walks. Her fingers swell, constricted by her rings.

"Actually, I was thinking about certain economic indicators for the international plastic market."

"You were thinking about your past. What were you thinking about it?"

He shrugs even though she can't see him. "It's long lost." He sidesteps something whipping across the trail into the brush.

Something reptilian probably. "I was thinking," he says, naming something safe, "of snipes."

"Oh," she says. "Snipes. We went on a snipe hunt once." She talks to the left side so he can see part of her cheek. "At Lake Mead. The bigger kids gave us paper bags and parked us there, told us to wait for these enormous birds." She shapes one with her arms. "We waited for hours before someone came and told us we were wasting our time."

"Hours?"

"Well," she concedes. "Maybe forty-five minutes."

"Snipes don't even live in Nevada," he says. "That's why you were wasting your time. Snipes live in Utah. And you could never catch one in a paper bag. We once gave a pack of Cub Scouts some gunny sacks, told them to wait on the hillside. We gave them a nicely detailed description of a snipe. Scales. Big nose. Stringy neck. Gold-plated molars. Everything we could think of. We told the kids to crouch down on a rock with the gunny sacks open and to whistle as high as they could. Snipes have very acute hearing, you know. If you whistle just the right notes, the snipes will run into the gunny sacks. Know what one of the kids said?"

"What?"

"'What's a gunny?'"

Elaine laughs. "Gunnies are even bigger than snipes, you should have told them. They eat goats."

"After which they burp and belch and suck blood," says Rob.

They are moving along the trail fairly fast now. Most of the group is behind, but there are several fresh tread prints when the trail is dirt, not rock. The thin-ridged soles are Terrill's. He and Andy spurted off as soon as they'd tied up their boats. The New Jersey soil engineer, Jerry P., had galloped after. Rob wanted to, Elaine is right, but Terrill—born-again blowhard, instinct epitomized—it's bad enough to watch him perform in public. Rob didn't think he could handle a private showing. Besides, Elaine keeps going distant on him. He wants to stick around. "Hmm," he says to her back, "what was easier to believe in—Joseph Smith and visiting angels or snipes and gunnies?"

A knee-high boulder blocks the trail. She sits on it, swings her legs over. "Not a fair choice," she says. "We didn't grow up singing songs about snipes every Sunday." She brushes off the back of her shorts, but since her hands are dirty, she makes the smudge worse. "Hey," she turns back after a few steps, "I still believe in gunnies."

This is a comfortable little canyon, he thinks. The main gorge isn't intimate and overgrown like this. It's vast, indifferent in its millions of years, the perfect antidote to human pride. Yet somehow the natives believed they mattered, mattered enough for gods to seek out and punish them. On the canyon walls, the Havusupai stone babies; in the depths of the gorge the remains of a retributive, earth-swallowing flood. Some tribes, he has read, have thought the Colorado their own road to hell. Some have believed in a god who inundated the road to Paradise—so human beings wouldn't try to sneak over the boundary.

According to the boatmen, most obstreperously Terrill, the whole Grand Canyon *is* Paradise, not the way to or the way from. Paradise. It sounds like the name of an Atlantic City amusement park. Mormons believe Paradise is a kind of check point in an endless cross-country race. He tries to remember the party line. Christ preaches there to the dead. Folks already prepared and repentant jog on towards a heaven which is itself a parcourse to another trail to—. Rob ducks under an ocotillo branch that Elaine has cleared with an inch to spare. Mormon Paradise isn't like Jewish Paradise, at least according to the Singer stories Elaine likes to read aloud. Nor like those other pastoral places, banana pudding in the sky and all.

He kicks at one of Terrill's thin-ridged sole prints. Earth, of course, is an exhausting place too, even for ex-Mormons, if there really is such a thing. Rob has suspected for some years now that there isn't. Alienated, repudiated, even excommunicated—which he isn't and doesn't want to be, Mom would suffer too much, maybe even he would suffer—there never is a final break. His boss doles out cocaine and Rob not only shakes his head, the small white cups make him think of the sacrament and he shudders inside. He doesn't contribute to, can't even laugh at the office lunch discussions of the Hindu sex positions. And before he met Elaine he had a very nice, very bright, very pagan girlfriend whom he saw only once after that first night at Jody's and that once to tell her goodbye. Elaine had a chance of understanding, he figured, about the faith that no longer securely folded him.

He bumps into her now, not noticing until the back of her head hits his chest that she has stopped. She takes a quick step forward and points at the cliff ahead. "Where'd the trail go?"

He looks around. "Over there. They said we'd be fording the creek. This must be the place." He repeats that with a gravelly voice. "This *is* the place." Elaine is unamused. Grimacing, he plunges into the water. It reaches his waist.

"It's deep," she says.

"Come on. You're the swimmer. Anyway I'm waiting for you."

She takes a few steps in, is up to her chest. "It's cold!" A few more steps and he grabs her outstretched arm. The rocks feel slick and spherical; they teeter on them as they push against the water and across the current. He boosts her up to the opposite bank to the trail. The wet shorts wrinkle around her bottom. The lower half of the daypack is wet. And probably the camera. He sighs. Oblivious, she trots on ahead, squeaking water out of her running shoes.

She bought those shoes a few years ago, has used them for everything but running. The plan was to try a mile or two in the mornings with him. She never really got into it. "It's not any fun," she'd say. "I'd rather ride the rec club Exercycle. At least I can read while I'm pedaling." She took up racquetball for a while, with Jody, but that didn't work out either. She finally settled on swimming—the one sport he dreads—maybe since the kayak splintered in Logan Canyon. She's good at it, too, likes the feel of the water on her body, she says, likes the stretch. She comes home late from work three days a week, hair wet and dark, slicked back behind her ears or tied in two stubby bunches at the sides of her face. "Two kilometers," she says, "or "Can do the butterfly ten minutes straight now." When she's pregnant, she tells him—they're talking about it, maybe next year—she'll be able to swim up until the last moment.

In front of them a sneeze punctuates the silence—Andy grinning and wiping his nose on his bare, brown arm. "Allergies," he sniffs, "to spring things. Flowers. Pollens." He blow his nose into a blue bandanna he pulls out of a tight pocket in his cutoffs.

"You already been up to Moony Falls?" Elaine asks.

"Just patrolling the trail. You found where to cross, I guess." He grins again, wide and toothy. He has a deep scar next to his right eye and it crosses with wrinkles when he smiles. "I'd better get back to the ford," he says. "Didn't mean to let you cross on your own." He sidles past.

"I like Andy," Elaine says when she judges he is out of earshot.

"You like everyone."

"No I don't. I don't like Lona much."

'Why not?" *He* doesn't like Lona because she's so severe, frenetic, so narrow-hipped, tight-lipped, but Elaine often talks to her at dinner. He thought of them as friends.

Elaine bends down and peers at a big-petalled orange mallow. "Maybe," she says finally, "because I'm something like her. That's a pretty common reason for disliking people. We dislike people we can compare ourselves with. Isn't that why *you* dislike," she pauses shrewdly, "certain people?" When he is silent, she straightens up, looks at him, ambles on.

To himself he thinks, me, comparing myself with that bigmouthed boatman? Terrill. What do we have in common? Even his name sounds manufactured, Hollywoodish, like the names of the women he is always, according to him anyway, humping, Tiffanies and Melissas and Jessicas and Kims. But he is good with the oars. Rob can tell by the way the other boatmen act. And he's got the women hypnotized. Even Elaine, who's usually distrustful of muscle men and Jesus freaks.

A Jesus freak. That at least is original, Rob thinks. It is so original that Terrill couldn't have made it up. It doesn't complement the Hemingway he-man crap. He must really believe it. Well. He slaps at another insect. Most of us did. Once.

There are shrill shouts on the trail ahead. Elaine turns around, looks at him. "What's that?" she asks.

"Snipes," he says.

The whoops take on bodies, a clump of khaki-clad kids with wet, rolled-down socks. "Hey mister," says the first one, a blond boy of about twelve whose shirt, still buttoned at the waist, hangs down about his shorts. "How far to the river?"

"Two miles," Rob says, "maybe three. Where'd you come from?"

Information acquired, the kid isn't interested in chitchat. He whistles at the Scouts bunching up behind him. "Two more miles, guys!" He shoots past. The others bump along after.

Twenty years ago, Rob thinks, Mom would iron his army drab uniform and mustard scarf so he could march like a little Nazi in a downtown parade or pant, too warm, on a mountain hike, or scrabble with similarly suited little fellows in the church parking lot. On the trail ahead, a sweating man in a large uniform leans against a big rock. His hair is stuck to his forehead. He seems to be breathing too hard to talk. He raises his eyebrows in a question and motions with his head the direction of the boys. Rob and Elaine nod, respecting his silence. He sighs and raises a foot, clumps heavily down the trail.

"If he's in such bad shape going downhill," Rob steps around a hedgehog cactus, "he'll probably have a coronary on the way back up."

"You could be a scout leader," she says.

"Huh?"

"I mean if we ever became Mormons again. I don't think scout leaders have to believe anything so long as they can tie knots."

Rob stops, stunned. "What are you talking about?" he starts to say, but distracted by a redbud tree, she is fishing the camera out of the daypack.

Her forehead creases, the foretelling of tears. "It's wet." She hands the camera to him.

"I should have carried it," he says as gently as he knows how but not gently enough.

She sucks in both lips. "Don't you take the blame. You'll just resent it when you start thinking about it. It's *my* fault." She sounds almost proud. "I'm sorry." She doesn't sound sorry. "I was careless." She pronounces "careless" as if it were two words.

"You weren't careless," he says. "You were just short." He pushes the camera back into her pack, brushes her hair aside and touches her neck. "Come on. Someone'll catch up."

"So what?" Her voice is strained.

"It's nice to have a few hours alone. You handle communal living better than I do. You had that kibbutz experience."

"Anyone who can live wedged in among ten million people for nine years ought to be able to handle twenty for two weeks." She takes long steps away from him. "Listen," she says. "Must be Beaver Falls."

The trail forks, the lower path ending at the base of a dozen short flat cascades terracing the widened river. The less-traveled path climbs the cliff, where shirtless, sunning like a large lizard, Terrill perches on a rock. "Hey," he sits up on his haunches, "wanna swim up to the second floor?"

"I thought you were hiking to Moony," Rob says.

Terrill closes his eyes and smiles. "Hiked up a few miles," he says, "to show Jerry the way. Thought I'd come back and show you the intermediate sights."

Elaine's eyes are bright. "What's over there?"

"More falls," Terrill says. "Prettier ones. Come on. I'll show you."

Elaine dumps the backpack with the ruined camera on a rock, peels off her already wet shorts and shoes, and wades into the same river she had nervously crossed below.

"Isn't it still cold?" Rob says.

"No. More sun here." She is suddenly gone, having apparently stepped off an underwater ledge. She reappears, sputtering, giggling, her hair molded to her head. "Don't you want to come?"

He doesn't, but Terrill is standing, overlooking the whole scene, so he shucks shoes and shirt and steps into the water. Elaine splashes over the rock rim that forms the low falls, her T-shirt sticking to her back. Now she is breast-stroking easily in the pool beyond.

Suddenly he feels nothing beneath his feet. He panics. The banks are close, he tells himself, he can always swim that far, but the water is so cold he can't breathe right when he tries the crawl. Elaine is in the middle of the pool now, paddling and shouting up at Terrill. "Now what?"

"You okay, Rob?" Terrill asks. He peers down from his cliff.

With wild strokes, Rob pulls himself over the bank and climbs up. "Too cold for me," he shivers. "I'll wait here."

Terrill nods. Then he plummets into the water, sneakers first. He bobs up next to Elaine. "Come on!" he says and swims off against the narrow rush of water. She follows. They are out of sight in a second. The churning water drowns out all sounds beyond. There goes my wife, Rob thinks, in her underpants, with a boatman. He settles on a rock and lets his feet sink into the mud. Briefly fascinated and repelled, he analyzes his own fear, envy, shame, disgust, relief. Then he thinks about practical things. He might as well try to get back to the main trail before anyone else arrives to see him stranded, abandoned.

If he sticks to the edge of the pond, hangs onto the sides, he can probably avoid the drop-off. The ragged rocks jab at his feet and dimple his hands, but he makes it to the base of the falls without getting his head wet. Sitting on a rock next to Elaine's shorts, he extracts the camera from her daypack and examines it. Maybe a good shop can do something. Some things can be repaired. He pulls on a sock. There is a trickle of blood along the side of his left arch. He massages his foot. Most wounds heal. He laces up his shoes.

There are sounds from the trail. Others are coming up the lower fork. It's plump Marie, glistening in her nylon running suit and a dull accountant whose name he can never remember.

"Been swimming, I see," the accountant says. "Where's Elaine?"

"She swam up to the back falls with Terrill."

"Didn't you try it?" asks Marie.

"I'm going to hike on up," Rob says. "Up towards the reservation. Maybe I'll be able to see them from the cliffs." He doesn't think of this until the instant he's said it. "Besides, I want to see Moony Falls."

Marie is shedding her shoes as he starts out on the upper fork. He pauses on the cliff side and looks down over the pool. He can't see the narrow passageway to the upper falls from here. The gravel slides under his feet. He leans into the mountain. Some of the rocks look and feel as hard as the side of a skyscraper, some crumble like rotten wood. All are dry, hot, and old, so old they obliterate the possibility of belief. And yet for centuries the men who walked this wilderness believed.

He hears a shout and looks down at the bank where he had pulled himself out of the pool. Marie is sitting there, embracing herself with her arms. "It's too cold," she yells. She has on a swimming suit top or a dark blue bra, he can't tell which. Her skin is pink, burning.

"And too deep," he shouts down. "And too wet." He turns back to the faint trail. A lizard skitters into a creosote bush. A thin-ridged print points the way, maybe, who knows, to Paradise.

Paradise Paved

ELAINE SWALLOWED DOWN DOWN DOWN HER FEAR. There, it was there someplace ricocheting around inside her ribs. She couldn't tell anybody, certainly not Stevie and Ben, who were wrestling over Stevie's last Tootsie Roll in the back seat. If she told them, they'd beller and she'd have to think of some way to calm them down. She stared out the front window of the Pontiac, across the shimmery asphalt parking lot to the supermarket.

Mama and Daddy had disappeared through those doors more than an hour ago. She'd kept track on her Minnie Mouse watch. An hour and fifteen minutes.

And she just knew they weren't coming back.

"E-laine!" whined Stevie. "Ben's pinching me." He kicked the back of her seat, Mama's seat really—Elaine had climbed over as soon as Mama had handed her the bag of Tootsie Rolls; hissed, "Be decent to each other"; and closed the door behind her. Elaine had divided the candy—which Ben gobbled up first—and settled down to read her *Archie and Veronica* comic book while her brothers read *Superman* and *Donald Duck*. But they were all fast readers, even Stevie, who was just six, and by now they had read each other's comic books and eaten all but that one Tootsie Roll and were feeling cramped and hot in the car even though they'd rolled the windows down all the way.

"E-laine!" Stevie yelled again.

She turned around. "Stop it!" she shouted. Ben paused for an instant, then resumed secretive manipulations of Stevie's thigh. "Ben!" She reached over and tried to pull his hand away.

"When are they coming back?" Stevie spluttered. "Why are they so long?"

"They're always long," Elaine said, but it seemed to her they weren't always *this* long. What could they be doing in Safeway all this time? She knew that, unlike the little grocery store in Boulder City, the big Las Vegas grocery stores had slot machines, and Mama saved up her nickels to play them. But an hour and fifteen minutes?

She peeled a big red star off the back of her left hand, the one Miss Hunsaker had stuck on this morning to reward her for playing Miss Hunsaker's favorite song, "Deep Purple," without one mistake. "Listen," Elaine said, "if you stop fighting, I'll tell you a story."

"'Bout what?" asked Ben. He finally let go of Stevie's leg. Stevie started unwrapping the last Tootsie Roll.

"Well," Elaine said, "about angels."

"Angels," said Stevie, taking a big bite. "Good."

"What kind of angels?" asked Ben.

"Boxcar angels," Elaine said.

For an instant, Stevie and Ben both sat still.

"Boxcar angels don't exactly live in boxcars." Elaine pulled a stick of gum out of her shorts pocket and divided it in two. "Here." She handed the pieces over the seat.

"Angels live in heaven," Stevie said, swallowing the last of the Tootsie Roll and stuffing in the gum.

"But boxcar angels spend a few days every month hiding out on freight trains. That way they can see the world from down here and see how they can help people. People don't even know they are angels until afterward."

"Do they have wings?" asked Stevie.

"They hide their wings. They wear big coats. And hats to hide their halos. Anyway, once upon a time, there was a girl who was almost ten years old—"

"Once upon a time means it isn't true," Ben said. "And in Sunday School they said that angels don't really have wings."

"Well, this is *my* story, not a Sunday School story. *My* angels have wings. Anyway, this girl—her name was Joya—she lived in a trailer with her mother and her little brother and her cat and they hardly had any money and they all slept in one bed."

"Joya's a funny name," said Ben.

"I wish we had a cat," said Stevie.

"And when it got to be Halloween, Joya didn't have a costume for the carnival at school. She hated to tell her mother because her mother worked so hard, she was a waitress at the donut shop, and she didn't have time to make Joya a costume, so Joya went to the store and looked at the costumes you could buy. There was a skeleton suit, all black except for the shiny white bones that glowed in the dark, and there was a pirate outfit and a cowgirl outfit and some princess outfits with crowns and net. Joya wanted to be a cowgirl and she looked real hard at the cowgirl costume box. Her brother had a cowboy hat and a cap gun she could probably borrow. But she didn't have a vest or a skirt with fringe or boots."

"This story sounds a lot like Cinderella," said Ben.

"Just wait," Elaine said. "So Joya went home and she got her most worn-out skirt from her closet and she took the kitchen scissors and she cut up the bottom so it kind of looked like fringe."

"Uh oh," said Stevie.

"When her mother came home from the donut shop, she saw Joya cutting up her skirt on the kitchen table, and she got really mad. Joya only had three skirts, and now one of them was ruined. Just then there was a knock on their trailer door, and a big wide woman in a gold cape and a big hat said, 'Do you happen to have a plaid skirt with a raggedy bottom? I'm on a scavenger hunt, and if I could find a plaid skirt with a raggedy bottom, I'd have everything I need. I'd win. And I'd give the person who gave me the plaid skirt with the raggedy bottom four big bags of groceries and three wool blankets and two Halloween costumes."

"That's dumb," said Ben.

"When are Mama and Daddy going to come back?" asked Stevie.

Well, thought Elaine, they might come back. After all, they wouldn't leave the car, would they?

ELAINE STRAPPED MINDY INTO HER CARSEAT, THEN handed her the plastic tub of Rice Chex that was supposed to keep her happy during the church meetings, if they'd stayed. "Don't wolf them down," Elaine said. "Eat them one at a time."

"Little squares," said Mindy, who was used to Cheerios. "Good."

Elaine climbed into the front seat. Rob was already behind the wheel.

"I don't know," he said, loosening his tie. "I don't think I can do it. Can you?"

"We should probably try it more than one Sunday. Maybe it was just the speakers today." She shook off her shoes onto the floor. "We could try a different place. How about Pasadena? There are more colleges in Pasadena, and it's about the same distance."

"It wasn't just the speakers. It was all the people around us. Young marrieds like us. They are probably *very* nice people, they probably would bring us lasagna and brownies and help us unpack the U-haul if they knew we were just moving in." He sighed. "They're so sunny and cheerful and sure of themselves. I could tell. They believe it all—they even *know* it is true, Angels and gold plates and stone tablets and burning bushes and everything else. And I know it's *not* true."

"Well," Elaine said, "I don't even know it's not true. I don't know anything. I never knew anything. But I *hoped* it was true once. And you did too."

Rob closed his eyes and nodded. Elaine chewed on her lower lip. "Maybe I still hope that. And maybe some of *them* are like us, underneath." She grinned. "It's just that it's hard to trust all those blondes with gorgeous tans." She fastened her seat belt and yanked on her too-short skirt. "I kept looking around the chapel, and it seemed to be getting smaller and smaller. Then I got a cramp in my foot."

Rob sighed. "Well, I know it's for Mindy that we were going to try it, but let's rethink this. We're going to tell her that a lot of this is malarkey but it's good to have a community and heritage? So she can go to meetings, but she should keep her mouth shut?"

"Maybe she won't think it's malarkey. Maybe she'll be a true bleached believer."

"Hungry," said Mindy, holding out her empty tub. "More little squares."

"Is that someone coming?" asked Rob. A man in a light suit was walking across the parking lot. Rob stepped on the gas and backed the car into the street. Elaine smiled at the man, who may or may not have intended to talk with them.

"I liked singing the hymns," she said as she opened up the Rice Chex. "I love 'The Spirit of God Like a Fire Is Burning.'"

"Yeah," Rob said. "Those Hosannas are great. Let's teach Mindy the best hymns."

"More little squares," said Mindy.

"WHERE WERE YOU?" MAMA ASKS WHEN ELAINE OPENS THE heavy passenger door of the ancient Oldsmobile, the one Mama stopped driving, thank heaven, three years ago, before she broke her hip and forgot how to walk. "Why did you leave me alone?" Her voice is high and hysterical.

"I just ran into the clinic to get their wheelchair, Mama." She clamps the wheelchair brakes, less stiff than those of Mama's own heavier wheelchair, which Elaine had laboriously heaved into the trunk back at Mama's condo garage. "It's faster to use their chair. I was only gone a couple of minutes. Here. Let's get you out." Mama swivels awkwardly towards the door. Elaine bends her knees, braces her back, and puts her arms under her mother's arms. "Hang onto me," she says, and gets her up and rotated. "Now sit."

"Everything's so much work." Mama reaches for her black purse. "The simplest things are so much work."

Sometimes Elaine contradicts her. Today she just wheels her into the clinic, gets the medical card out of her mother's purse, and presents it to the receptionist.

"Shirley, how are you?" Doctor Teal, her brown hair pulled back in a shiny tail, plops onto the examining room stool so she's eye level with Mama. She knows she has to speak loudly.

"I'm rotten," says Mama. "How are you?"

"I'm fine," laughs Doctor Teal. "But why are you rotten?"

"Listen," Mama says, "if you were 88, you'd feel rotten too."

"Eighty-nine," says Elaine. "You're 89 now, Mama."

"That's even more rotten," says Mama.

"Do you hurt anyplace?" asks Doctor Teal.

"I hurt everyplace."

Doctor Teal looks concerned. "Where exactly?"

"You name it," Mama says.

"She says her knees and legs and feet mostly," Elaine offers.

"And my hands and shoulders," says Mama.

Doctor Teal stands and puts her stethoscope on Mama's rounded back. "Take a big breath for me now." She listens. "Sounds fine. You're quite a remarkable lady, Shirley. What's the secret of your good health and longevity?"

"Clean living," Mama says promptly. "No cigarettes, no alcohol, no caffeine." She looks darkly at Elaine who uses, she knows, though in moderation, alcohol and caffeine.

Doctor Teal pats Mama's arm. "Where are you living?"

"My own home."

"It's a condo with elevators and wide doors. They sold their house in Boulder and moved to Vegas the year before my dad died," Elaine says. "We have someone to live here with her. A wonderful woman, Conchita."

"A busybody," says Mama. "And she picks her nose."

"Where do you live, Elaine?"

"In L.A. But I'm here for a week at least every other month."

"Have you thought of moving her down there with you?"

"She ought to move up here with me," says Mama. "I've got plenty of room."

Elaine sighs. "She made me promise years ago that we wouldn't take her out of her home. In L.A. she'd have to be in an assisted-living facility. We don't have any bedrooms on the first floor." She shrugs. "Our lives are in California. My husband is still working. And we help our daughter with her new baby. They live close to us."

"Everybody's just waiting for me to die," says Mama. "Me, too. I'm more eager than any of them."

"You've probably got years yet, Shirley." Dr. Teal holds her hand, and for a moment Mama softens.

"Know how much I weighed when I was born?" Mama says.

"That's not in your chart."

"I weighed 13 pounds, 4 ounces. Ended my mama's birthing days." She squeezes Dr. Teal's hand. "I had a hard time getting into this world, and I'm having a hard time getting out."

"That's because you aren't ready."

Mama grunts. "Every night I pray the Lord to take me. I'm ready."

MAMA TAKES LITTLE NAPS IN HER RECLINING CHAIR IN the den. She can sleep and still hold onto the newspaper or the pen she uses on the crosswords or the TV remote. Elaine waits till Mama wakes up, then sits on the piano bench to strap on her sandals. "I'm going down to the grocery store. I want to fill up your larder so that you and Conchita won't have to worry much about food till the next time I come."

"We used to do that two-year food storage program," says Mama. "But you can't do that in a condo."

"This will be for about two months." Elaine poises her pencil over a pad. "I've made a list. Do you have any special requests?"

"Cashews," says Mama. "And root beer."

Conchita is watching television in her room when Elaine knocks on her door and tells her where she's going. Then she drives the massive Oldsmobile over to Safeway and parks near the cart-return. She relaxes once she passes through the automated doors into the cool store. Las Vegas is much hotter than L.A.

A woman who looks familiar is holding up a large cantaloupe and sniffing the stem end. Someone from school maybe—Elaine hasn't been good about keeping in touch with her high school and college friends, hasn't gone to any reunions. She smiles at the woman in a vague, noncommittal way.

"Elaine," the woman says.

The name comes to her. No, Lou Anne's partner on the college debate team. "Susan."

"Are you living here?" Susan puts the cantaloupe in her basket.

"No," says Elaine. "But I'm here a lot now. I've got a high-maintenance mama. And you? Have you been in Vegas all this time?"

Susan nods. "Twenty-five years in the classroom. Married the principal my fifth year."

"You teach English."

"English, yes." Susan shifts her weight to her other foot. "Does it show?"

Elaine laughs. "I remember how literary you were." Susan looks literary still, with her narrow, Virginia Woolf face, her little round glasses. "Do you have kids close by?"

"A boy at UNLV. Girls have flown the coop. Both married, Kitty in Phoenix, Renee in Houston. Five grandkids." She shows the fingers on her right hand, then becomes serious. "Remember Lou Anne?"

"Lou Anne Garston. Sure. I thought of her when I saw you."

"Lou Anne Raven now. She has ALS. She can't even talk. It's so sad. And her youngest is only a junior in high school. And A.J. Hunsaker, remember him?"

The name takes Elaine by surprise. "I remember A.J."

"He died last month. Shot himself."

"No."

"Yes. You had something going with him, didn't you?"

"We both worked on the campus newspaper. We ran around a little together. His aunt was my piano teacher back in Boulder. He shot himself?"

"It was on the front page of the *Sun*. He was the president of the Rotary Club or something like that. They found him in his office. Maybe he had cancer. I think Lou Anne wishes she could shoot herself."

"The Rotary Club!" Elaine says. "But we were all such radicals!"

"Well, shooting himself sounds radical. But nothing else. I was driving behind him one day about a year ago. He was in one of those humungous SUVs, the kind that could do combat with a tank. And on the back were all these revolting bumper stickers, NRA, Armed with Pride, stuff like that." She stopped talking. "You aren't into that now, are you?"

"Lord, no."

"And someone told me he had signs on his lawn, Silent Scream sort of thing, big pictures of aborted fetuses. Neighbors were very unhappy, even the antichoice ones. No one wants to buy on a block with a yard like that. Hey," says Susan, "I don't have anything frozen yet, and you have an empty basket. Let's go next door to the smoothie place. We've got at least a quarter-hour of catching up to do, and I have a bad back. I can walk, but not stand."

"Fifteen minutes," says Elaine. "I can do fifteen minutes."

IT TAKES MORE THAN FIFTEEN MINUTES. AS SHE LOADS the car with groceries, as she drives back to the condo, as she hauls bags into the kitchen, Elaine thinks about A.J. Hunsaker. A.J. Hunsaker was the first guy who asked her to go to bed with him, the first guy she'd told no. She had been surprised—guys then didn't just go around asking things like that. She'd not been at all tempted. She'd been a little Mormon girl, after all, even if she was a pacifist with long, straight hair, who plunked out chords on her guitar and sang "If I Had a Hammer."

Conchita finds her stuffing orange juice concentrate cans into the freezer. "Your mother upset. She worry about you." She points with her chin to the groceries. "I put away."

Elaine scurries into the den. "Hi Mama," she says brightly. "I ran into an old friend—took a little longer than I'd planned."

"I never thought," says Mama, "that I would see the day when a child of mine would abandon me."

"Mama!" Elaine says. "I just went to the grocery store."

"Would leave me here alone. I can't be alone."

Elaine pulls the piano bench over close to Mama's feet. "You weren't alone." She sits. "Conchita was here. We wouldn't leave you alone."

"Alone," Mama says again. "I'm always alone. When is your daddy coming back?"

Elaine stares at Mama. She *looks* normal.

"Mama," she says. "Daddy isn't coming back. He can't. Don't you remember?"

Mama starts crying. "I get so confused," she says.

"He would come back if he could. He wouldn't leave you by yourself if he were alive."

"I'm so alone," she sobs. "Don't you leave me alone too."

"I'm never very far away. Just an hour by airplane. I come often."

Mama stops crying. "I know." She swallows. "I want you to do something for me. I want you to promise me something."

Elaine feels wary. "What's that, Mama?"

"Promise me."

"Promise you what, Mama?"

"Promise me you'll go to church again the way you used to when you were young."

"Oh Mama," Elaine says. "None of us can be the same as when we were young. I could just as easy climb the monkey bars at the elementary school, I could just as easy take tap dancing lessons again as I could be the little girl who believed everything everyone told me."

Mama sniffs. "You never believed everything everyone told you."

"I tried. I wanted to."

"If you don't promise, I can't die. I want for us to all be together in heaven. I've got to stay alive till you go back to church."

Elaine laughs. "But Mama, I don't *want* you to die. You've just given me another reason to *not* go back to church."

"I don't think Rob would mind your going." Mama rarely mentions Rob. She pauses. "If you really cared for me, you'd do it."

"People can't believe things just because they love someone who believes."

"If your Daddy had believed, then maybe you'd believe."

"Now Daddy," Elaine says, "he adored you, but he couldn't believe all the things you believe."

"If I'd been a better mother, you'd believe."

"Mama! That's a terrible thing to say about both of us. You're a wonderful mother. And I'm a pretty good mother too. We care for our children, we teach them the best we know how, the best we can." Elaine fusses with the maroon fleece blanket over Mama's legs. "You know, I'm glad you believe even if I can't. And if you're right about things, if you're right about heaven, then you can pray me and Daddy right into heaven with you." And if you're wrong, Elaine thinks, you'll never know. "Look," she says, "you got two out of three church-going kids. In our family that's probably a record."

Mama's chin wobbles. "But girls matter more. Nobody expects girls to leave."

"All of Aunt Mildred's girls left. Four of them."

Suddenly Mama looks weary. "Hey," Elaine says, "speaking of family, I haven't shown you these pictures of the world's cutest grandbaby." She reaches for her shoulder bag, extracts a fat envelope. "Look." She sticks big glossy prints in front of Mama's face. "Here Rob is holding her." She looks at her watch. "He's tending her right now too, so Mindy can work a few hours a day. And here she is on Greg's shoulders—he's such a doting dad." She smiles at another print. "Look. Isn't she adorable? That's the outfit that I got her with the money you sent."

Mama glances at the photograph. "She looks a little like you," she says.

Elaine gathers up the pictures and drags the piano bench back.

"Whatever happened to Miss Hunsaker? You remember—my piano teacher?"

Mama tries to concentrate. "I haven't heard anything about her for a long time. I don't think she ever married. Guess she's still in Boulder. There was another Hunsaker though, one you knew in college, and something happened to him."

"Her nephew. A.J. He died." Elaine sits up straight. "Do you know what I remember about Miss Hunsaker? It was in the sixth grade, and Mrs. Gould couldn't teach the last month because she was too pregnant, and they didn't let too-pregnant women teach grade school then, and so they got Miss Hunsaker to substitute for all of May. I don't think Miss Hunsaker liked kids much, and I know she didn't like teaching the sixth grade. Anyway, one morning she stumbled into the classroom in a long, yellow, organdy kind of dress and high-heeled sandals. She kept giggling. And then the principal and the fifth grade teacher came in and took her off to the teacher's room, and when she came back, they'd cut about two feet off the bottom of her dress and probably filled her up with coffee. Do you remember that?"

Mama cocks her head. "I think so. It was a scandal."

"It was! Hey! How would you like to drive over to Boulder tomorrow? Look around the town?"

"I'm so hard to move," says Mama. She looks at her legs, now elevated, under the fleece.

"We can stay in the car if you want. Just see how the old house looks. My schools. Maybe Miss Hunsaker's house. The tennis courts where we used to roller skate. Daddy's grave in the cemetery."

"And the church," says Mama. "If you don't mind hauling me around." She points to her wheelchair. "Did I tell you I want to be buried in that chair?"

"You did, Mama."

"You're going to tell me it's not possible, aren't you? That's what Steve says."

"He doesn't know everything. Maybe we could get a custom-built coffin. It'd cause quite a stir at your funeral." They both laugh.

Elaine opens up the piano bench. "Want me to play something for you?"

Mama closes her eyes and nods. Inside the piano bench are old piano books and older sheet music. Elaine pulls out, then puts back "On Wisconsin" and "Shrimp Boats Is A-Coming" and a blue hymnal. She flattens "Deep Purple" against the music stand and sits down.

"When the deep purple falls," she sings to the chords, "over sleepy garden walls—" She can almost see, standing at her right elbow, Miss Hunsaker, a pen in her right hand, a short, fat glass of something clear and tinkly in her left. When she would lean over Elaine to correct her hand position or draw arrows to the problem notes, Elaine could smell Miss Hunsaker's strong, juniperish breath.

"And the stars begin to flicker in the sky—" Miss Hunsaker wore gauzy, low-necked blouses, even at 9:30 on Saturday mornings. "Through the mist of a memory, you wander back to me—" Elaine looks over at Mama, dozing in her chair. "Breathing my name with a sigh."

Elaine plays on, humming the next verse. Conchita peers in, surveys the room, disappears with a quick wave. In the mist of a memory, Miss Hunsaker also waves, waves with her angel wings, waves with her glass of gin, and winks at Elaine. Then she too disappears.

The River Rerun

Morning 3, Nankoweap camp

ACROSS THE RIVER, SHE SEES A BIG BROWN LUMP SHAMBLE over to the water's edge. She wants it to be graceful, sleek, to glide through the water, not lumber like a bear on the land. Elaine can see it through the right lens of her binoculars. It is what she longed to see thirty—thirty!—years ago, on that last trip down the Colorado. It is a beaver.

It does not make her heart hop.

The left lens of her binoculars fogged up yesterday, which wasn't supposed to happen since they are waterproof binoculars, good ones. They didn't have binoculars the other time. She and Rob smirked at the one person who did, the mousy woman who was always calling out bird names. They were young then; smirking came easily. The muscles of their mouths, the muscles in their legs, shoulders, backs—they all moved effortlessly, without consequence.

"Just got the permit, Aunt Elaine," Chip, Ben's boy, had said on the phone. "A cancellation. So I'm putting together a trip. Uncle Rob said you two always wanted to run the Colorado again, right? Now you're retired so you can. And I talked to my folks. They could come stay at your place that week and visit Grandma in the nursing home every day."

He thought of everything, Chip did. And Rob so wanted to go, to prove to himself that he could do it. Just getting on the J-Rig though made her wonder. They couldn't scramble onto the pontoons the way the others did. Rob could hop over from the rocks. Elaine's arms were pretty good, so she could haul herself up.

That first day, they saw condors through the binoculars, three of them, flying over the canyon, and she thought she might have spotted a nest. She passed the binoculars around—everyone wanted to see birds as big as gliders, a species that might—now—survive. Even Mike wanted to see, Mike who doesn't believe in evolution and extinction.

Yesterday they just rode small rapids, nothing more than Class 5's, and she doesn't think it was the water that clouded up the left lens. After all, the salesman said he cleaned his binoculars by putting them in the sink. Maybe it was the steam from her body in the sun.

It's early. The only other person up is pretty, pensive Olivia, wandering down by the river. In among the tamarisks, Rob and the others are still asleep, on cots, atop sleeping bags—it's warm here, it's June. Elaine woke to a chorus of canyon wrens and tottered off with the binoculars in search of them. She found one too, through her right lens, singing its heart out.

Mornings are the best time. It's the nights that she dreads, too stiff, too stimulated, too worried to sleep. Mom in the nursing home, sometimes happy, sometimes hating it. But maybe she'll behave for Ben and Bertie. At home Elaine doesn't sleep well either though it is soothing to have Rob next to her under the sheet instead of two feet away in a separate sleeping bag on the other cot. The first night, at South Canyon, Chip put their cots head to head because there was such a narrow spot for them.

Dear Chip brought the cots. They all, except Chip, who sleeps on the J-Rig, and Vin and Allie, who are very young and who can't stop touching each other, use cots. Vin and Allie set up their little camp as far away from the rest as possible. Could they have managed sex on a cot? Well, maybe on Mike's queen-size cot, the cot Tom and Vin scoffingly call "Princess." How old I am, Elaine thinks. Yesterday, in the late afternoon, when the others were hiking up to the Indian granaries, she and Rob stayed in camp, stripped off all their clothes in the warm sun, used the tepid water in Chip's sun shower bag and the cold water of the Colorado to wash off the sunscreen and sweat and sand. It wasn't the least bit sexy. Rob has those love handles and a bit of a belly; she would be thin but for the fat joints, and she has that wrinkly neck and ugly moles all over her torso and mottled thighs. And the steel-colored hair, cropped short, a helmet, Rob calls it. It's the same color as his beard. If someone had been spying from the brush, they would not, alas, have been titillated.

Thirty years ago, no one had cots, and almost everyone was titillated. Sex was a watery undercurrent beside the Colorado even though nobody actually did much, at least that she and Rob knew about. Too communal, too crowded. They have made a conscious effort on this trip not to bore the others with their memories. She has her old blue river guide still, with dates and notes. Saturday, while they were waiting at Lee's Ferry, she was chatting with the grey-bearded guy who brought Chip his back-up motor, and she asked him if he knew any of the boatmen and boatwomen from way back when—she was thinking of Terrill, wild-man Terrill with his peeling, muscular bare arms and his effusive tales of heroism—and the grey-bearded guy said Terrill lives in Flagstaff and still does an oar trip now and then. Elaine finds that extraordinary—that Terrill is still alive, that he hasn't perished in some South American revolution or been shot by a jealous husband.

Chip's is a small private trip—two aged relatives and five friends, not a commercial excursion like the one they did all those years ago though they and their fellow travelers were young then and expected to pitch in, loading and unloading morning and evening, and bailing out the water that filled the bottoms of the rafts in the rapids. The commercial trips they've seen this year—waiting at Lee's Ferry before set-in, at camps that they'd passed, on the river itself—seemed to cater to big groups of the recently retired, people as old as or even older than themselves. At Lee's Ferry, Elaine watched them wilting in the shade of their big bus or waiting in line at the cinderblock bathrooms, the last flush toilets anyone would see for some time. The women wore too much eye makeup and too tight tank tops and fluorescent flip-flops with plastic flowers. Later that day, coming behind them through Badger Creek rapid, Elaine saw that they were clinging to the ropes along the sides of two enormous motorized rafts, sporting, under the orange life jackets that everyone on the river wears, matching blue windbreakers. At one campsite, their guides, "caretakers," said Rob, had set up a neat row of matching tents.

"But *we* need care," she told Rob. So far Allie and Vin have unloaded their heavy dry bags in the evening and dragged them back down to the J-Rig in the morning. Elaine and Rob just watch as the others heave the bags off and on, and as Mike, who has taken on "groover" duty, sets up and dismounts the metal box-toilet. They wouldn't be able to straighten up the rest of the week if they tried to lift any of that stuff. They've mostly helped with meals—Chip's wife Kim had packed nine days of food, some frozen, in the big bins under the deck. The deck very cleverly doubles as the meal preparation table with fold-out legs, and they have big canvas chairs with drink holders that Rob and Elaine are in charge of setting up and folding and stuffing back into their sandy bags.

"So how long have you and Rob been together?" Elaine turns to see Olivia, who has soundlessly approached from the brush. She must have walked all the way around.

"Good morning." Elaine smiles at her, but Olivia doesn't smile back. "Thirty-three years. Before you were born." Olivia runs her fingers through her coppery hair. She hasn't tied it into a ponytail yet and stuck it through the hole in her cap. "Are you sleeping okay?" Elaine asks gently. Olivia looks as if she has been crying.

"Not really." She looks down at her purple-red toenails. "Tom's into this camping stuff. I'm not. He went with Chip down

Cataract Canyon last summer a couple of times. He didn't insist I go then, but the Grand Canyon, well, he says I have to do this. Chance of a lifetime and all." She pauses. "I miss Danielle. She's only six. She's with my folks in Grand Junction. I didn't know I wouldn't even be able to *call* her every night."

"Your camera," Elaine points to Olivia's wrist strap, "do you have any pictures of her?"

"Oh yeah," Olivia says. "Here. Look." There on the screen is a small girl, red-haired and light-skinned, hugging a large yellow dog. She looks to be about the same age as Elaine and Rob's first grandchild, darling Penny.

"She looks like you," Elaine says. "Who's taking care of the dog?"

"That's Barney." Olivia smiles at her camera. "Next-door neighbors. We haven't lived in Phoenix very long. Tom and Chip worked together in Grand Junction, but Tom got laid off last year—I guess he didn't impress the boss as much as Chip did—and now he works for his dad. Phoenix is okay, but it's so hot. Kids can't play outside until November. And we loved Grand Junction. And *my* folks are a lot more helpful than *his* folks." She glances at her watch. "Guess I'll go wake up Tom," she says. "Packing the dry bags is a real bore, isn't it?"

"Not the best part of the trip," Elaine agrees.

But not the worst either, she thinks as Olivia disappears into the mesquite.

Afternoon 4, Elves Chasm

ROB IS STILL ON THE J-RIG WITH CHIP, BUT THE OTHERS are on their way up, so Elaine adjusts her walking sticks and follows. In the blue river book, thirty years ago, she wrote, "Short Hike to Elves Chasm," but now she sees there isn't a trail. How do the others know where to go? Vin and Allie haven't been here before, but they set off at a run up the boulders as soon as they pulled in. Tom and Olivia followed them. Tom, at least, ought to know the way—he and Chip and Mike and some other he-men took the J-Rig through the Grand Canyon two years ago. Elaine is trying to scramble up the rocks behind Mike, her least favorite person in the group. Last night he told her that he has collected plenty of weather data for the past hundred years, and he sends it to school with his kids to prove to the teachers that the earth is getting colder, not warmer.

"I wish it were true," she told him.

"C'mon," he says now, glancing back over his shoulder at her. "This way."

And then he is gone and she can't decide which is *this* way. She opts for the flattest rocks and gasps as a lizard scuttles out of the path of her hiking stick. It's lovely here anyhow, even if she doesn't get to Elves Chasm. But maybe she'll intercept Chip and Rob when they start climbing.

She goes forward sometimes, backtracks sometimes, takes left turns, tries to go up. A cavern with water and ferns is very pretty, so she stops and drinks from her canteen. She is clearly lost, but she is exasperated, not afraid. Mike is a jerk. In the rapids he perches on the left pontoon just daring the waves to wash him into the river. She wishes they would.

Yesterday was the start of the big rapids, the big adrenalin rushes. Hance and Horn, and today, Hermit—she likes those breathy H names. And then Crystal. Olivia got hysterical at Crystal. Elaine had held her to calm her. She discovered it's hard to hug someone when you're both wearing life jackets.

She sees what could be a grassy trail back to the river. Around big rocks, she suddenly comes upon a pool with three people lazily kicking their feet in the water. They must be from the group of kayakers that passed them while they were having lunch. Kayaks on the Colorado. Elaine can hardly believe they would make themselves so vulnerable. The one in the khaki cap is a woman, and not a young woman either, maybe 45. Elaine waves at them. "This the way down?" she asks.

"Yeah. You on that big boat?" asks the woman. Elaine nods. "The one we saw hung up at Crystal?"

"Our nephew built that boat. He ran it onto a rock, and one of the guys jumped out to try to push us off, and we almost squashed him. He was okay though. But it took his wife a while to recover."

"Crystal's never easy," says the older of the men. "Usually too little water."

"How often have you done this?" Elaine asks. He holds up both hands, fingers extended.

"I've only done it four times," says the younger man. "Mom has done it seven."

Elaine gasps. "And I thought I was brave," she says, "just clutching the ropes."

SHE SETTLES HERSELF WITH HER BOOK IN THE SHADE near the J-Rig. During quiet times, she has been trying to read *Beyond the Hundredth Meridian*, but has had difficulty concentrating. John Wesley Powell was braver even than the kayakers. Uncharted territory. 1869. Wooden boats. One arm. John Wesley Powell might have needed a little help in getting up to Elves Chasm, except white men didn't know about Elves Chasm then. But the book says Powell was about Chip's age when he and his men tackled the Colorado, and he apparently hiked wherever his men hiked. She loves the story about his getting trapped in a side canyon, unable to go ahead or go back, and how he yelled out to George Bradley, who was always, it seems, rescuing the others, and Bradley, who didn't have a rope, lowered his own long underwear, which Powell lunged for and which helped him either up or down, the book doesn't say. Three of the men deserted Powell later though. And they probably didn't survive. Served them right, she thinks.

Of course Mom thinks *they've* abandoned *her*. "My kids stuck me in here," she tells people who visit the nursing home. "Don't get old. They treat you like trash." That's what she says when she's the most lucid. That's when she might hit an aide with her telephone or swear a blue streak at the nurse. She'd kick people if her legs still worked. When she's more confused, she loses her feistiness and seems helpless and pathetic. Elaine shuts her book and sighs.

Allie and Vin appear in front of her. "We were worried about you," they chorus. Vin adds, unnecessarily, "Everyone was up there but you."

Elaine shrugs. "I tried. I was following Mike, but he left me in the dust."

Allie shakes her head. Her hair is wet and kinky. "He shouldn't have done that," she says. "That's awful."

"It was probably too hard a scramble for me anyway," Elaine says. She must have inherited the martyr skills from Mom. "Did Rob make it?"

"Chip did have to help him," Vin says. "But he got there. You should've seen him jumping off."

"Tom got pictures," Allie says. "It's so beautiful. They'll show you when they get back."

"Did everyone jump in?" Elaine asks. She tries not to sound annoyed. Thirty years ago, the drop from the high hole in the rock was too scary for her. Rob had done it because he felt he had to. But at least then she got to see it, the narrow gorge, the cascades, the green, green pools, and she had paddled around in the water while the others jumped.

"Everyone leapt in," says Vin. "Even Olivia."

"But she didn't want to," says Allie. "Tom kind of made her."

"But she was glad once she did it," Vin says. Allie looks unconvinced.

The others are coming down the rocks. Rob and Chip are relieved and a little abashed, she thinks, to see her. "Where did you go?" they ask. "We figured you'd decided not to come."

"Just went up a little way."

"You should've seen Uncle Rob jump," says Chip.

"I couldn't have made it up there without Chip." Rob is clearly very pleased with himself. "He practically carried me. Where were you?"

She looks at him, then looks away. "I went to the mall," she says tartly, "and bought some mascara."

Night 6, National Canyon camp

OLIVIA HAS DISAPPEARED. TOM IS FRANTIC. HE AND CHIP are hiking up National Canyon, a big flashlight augmenting their headlamps. Vin and Allie and Mike are searching closer to the camp and up and down the river. Rob and Elaine hear them calling Olivia's name.

"Won't do much good to call," Rob says, "if she means to go missing." They are sitting in the canvas chairs close to the water's edge. It would be a pleasant night—mild breeze, clear sky studded with stars—if Tom hadn't come rushing back from their campsite and raised the alarm. Olivia had excused herself after dinner, didn't want to play "Murder" in the sociable circle around the pole lamp.

"She's not a happy woman," says Elaine.

"Are you a happy woman?"

Elaine thinks about this. She has thought about this a lot, especially since her newspaper folded, giving her time to think of all the connotations of that word "retire."

"Well," she says, "I wouldn't head up one of the side canyons by myself."

"So, if you could choose to live your life again, would you?"

"I guess," she says. "Yes. Sure. You would, wouldn't you?"

"Yeah." He runs his hand over hers. "Even if it doesn't make much sense."

"We've made it make sense."

"People like Mike don't have to do that, do they? Chip either. They just know there is a big purpose. They're probably reconciled to death. Find meaning in pain. All that." He clears his throat; Elaine thinks his voice catches. "Lucky bounders. Look how well my folks did after LaNell died, lots better than I did, and they're her parents. They *know* they'll see her again. They'll all be together in tidy tract houses in the sky."

"There's more to life than death," Elaine says. "Than facing death."

"Yeah, but some of those things are explained by religion too. Suffering. Injustice. Not explained satisfactorily, but, well, some people are satisfied, aren't they? Take your brothers. Steve. Ben. Ben and Bertie raised Chip to believe all that hooey, and they all claim to be happy. Do you think Mindy'd be happier if we'd raised her to be a believer?"

"I think Mindy's happy." Elaine sighs. "Who knows if someone else is happy or not? And *we* were raised to be believers. We just didn't keep believing." She sucks her lips in. "Bertie takes a lot of Zoloft. And look at Mom. Well, we function anyway. We aren't a dysfunctional family, are we?"

"No." He strokes her hand, fingers. "Your finger tips are cracking. Are you glad we came?"

"I'll tell you when we find Olivia. We *will* find her, won't we?"

"How far could she go?"

"Farther than she thought before this trip. I had to talk her into hiking up Havasu yesterday. She wanted to stay with us while the rest of them went. I knew *we* couldn't do it again, but I told her *she* could." She digs her feet into the sand. "I told her how gorgeous Beaver Falls are. You hiked all the way to Mooney back then. None of them made it to Mooney yesterday."

"Chip could've," Rob says, "if he didn't have to worry about everyone else. Maybe Olivia's scared of Lava tomorrow."

"We're all scared of Lava," Elaine says. "We're supposed to be scared of Lava."

"You're not as scared as last time."

"No," she says. "Even after Chip told us today how he flipped the J-Rig in Cataract Canyon last summer. I didn't know about that."

"He probably didn't tell Ben and Bertie."

She laughs. "Didn't tell them about that man who got tossed out and who ended up miles downstream and his wife who became unhinged, who'd blame her, who told Chip this wouldn't have happened if he had a prayer every morning before they set out. You know," she says, "we have faith. Mindy has faith. We just have faith in different things than Ben and Chip and especially Mike."

"Yeah." Vin is hallooing down the river. Way down. Allie and Mike must be with him. Chip told them to stay together.

Elaine opens her river book and sets her headlamp beam on the page. "Look," she says. "Thirty years ago, we camped here. It was the eleventh night, and we were going to be on Terrill's boat the next day. He got us so worked up about Lava!"

"Terrill," Rob snorts.

"Took us a lot longer on those oared rafts. It seems too easy with the J-Rig and a motor. Except when the motor kills, that's pretty unnerving."

"We don't have to bail. Water runs right off the deck. And that truck seat Chip has for us to sit on. This is the luxurious life."

"I don't know," she says. "My hips hurt all the time."

There is the strident sound of a whistle coming from up the side canyon. Chip has given Vin a whistle too. One blast means they've found Olivia and to return to camp. Two means "come."

Rob lets out a breath. "Now let's hope she's okay."

"She's okay," Elaine says, "physically."

Vin and Allie and Mike get back to the campsite first.

"I'm so glad." Allie sinks into a canvas chair next to Elaine and switches off her headlamp. "What could she be thinking of?"

"She's not thinking," Mike says.

"We've got to make her feel comfortable," Allie says. "Tell her we love her and everything. Don't tell her how she got us all worried sick."

"How she almost ruined our trip," Mike says.

"We don't know what happened," says Rob. "Let's make like she was just walking around, maybe on the way to the groover, and she couldn't find her way back."

"Right," Vin says.

Chip and the spotlight lead the way. Behind him, fierce little headlamps shining, the two others. Tom's arm is around Olivia. She is sobbing. Rob reaches them first. "It's so easy to get lost." He touches Olivia's shoulder. "We're just happy they found you." She stops crying for just an instant and looks at him, then buries her head in Tom's chest.

"We all need a good night's sleep," Chip says. "We've got a big day tomorrow."

Morning 7, Lava Falls

"VULCAN'S ANVIL," SAYS CHIP, FROM THE BACK OF THE J-Rig. He motions towards the black mound of lava in the river as they pass it. "Vulcan was the Roman god of fire."

"Live long and prosper," says Rob, doing the Vulcan salute.

"They're all too young to know *Star Trek,*" says Elaine, but Mike laughs. "Mr. Spock," he says. "I remember." Mike is in his regular spot, atop the left pontoon. Tom, who usually rides the right pontoon, is sitting on the deck, his arm around Olivia's waist. She is wearing dark glasses and looks at no one.

"Reruns," Rob whispers to Elaine. "Remember Mindy could do the Vulcan salute."

Chip pulls the J-Rig onto the rocks. "Mike and I'll scout Lava," he says, "so we can decide how to run her. You all sit tight." Mike ties up the boat, and the two of them trot down the rocky trail.

"So what are our chances of flipping?" Allie asks Tom.

"Minuscule. This is a *big* boat. And Chip knows what he's doing." He glances down at Olivia, but she doesn't acknowledge his attention.

"He did flip in Cataract," Allie reminds him. "On the upper Colorado. Were you with him then?"

"Naw," Tom says. "He had a group from his church. But that was Big Drops. They're more serious rapids than Lava."

"I didn't think anything was more serious than Lava," Allie says. "Chip even said a prayer this morning."

That was after everyone had finished their cold cereal and oranges. It had been a simple prayer for protection and guidance, and Chip hadn't mentioned Lava by name. The people who didn't say prayers were looking around at those who had their heads bowed—Chip, Mike, Tom, Olivia. "When I'm in a tight spot," Chip had said afterwards, "I say, 'Lord, if you get me out of this one, I'll never get back on the river again.' And the Lord always gets me out of trouble. And I always get back on the river."

It seems to take a very long time before Chip and Mike return. Vin has found a sack of cashews and has passed them around. He offers them to Chip when he bounds back onto the J-Rig.

"It's doable," Chip says. Mike unties the rope, pushes the J-Rig away from the rocks and jumps to his pontoon. "Now I don't want anyone on the pontoons," Chip says. I want you all on the deck, hanging onto the straps. Allie, you get onto the truck seat, and you too, Olivia, next to Elaine and Rob. Mike, Tom, Vin, here, in front of them." He has Olivia and Allie trade places, so Olivia and Elaine are in the middle, the safest spots. He winds an extra line on the deck for them to grab.

"What if you're bounced off the boat?" Allie asks.

"Then Tom or Mike will take over till I'm fished out," Chip says. "Everyone ready?"

He settles his cap back onto his head and starts up the motor. Elaine clenches the rope across her lap. With white knuckles Rob clutches the rope too.

"Wahoo," shouts Chip. "Wahoo!" shouts Mike. "Yeah," shouts Vin. "Go for it!" says Rob, not as loudly.

They are, for a moment, submerged in an enormous wave, then thrust above it, then slammed under water again. Elaine remembers to keep her eyes open. They burst through and are suddenly in calm water. All that anticipation and what did it take? Half a minute?

"Man!" Chip roars. "What a great run!" "Yeah, yeah, yeah!" howls Mike. They all laugh. Elaine squeezes Olivia's hand. She is laughing too.

Day 8, Separation Canyon

THEY'VE PULLED INTO SEPARATION CANYON FOR LUNCH. On the deck-table, Elaine and Rob have spread out the bread, mustard, cheese, lunchmeat, lettuce, oranges, Oreos; sliced the tomatoes, pickles. Mike builds an enormous sandwich with everything but oranges. The others laugh when he places two Oreos between his cheese and lunchmeat. "How you gonna get your mouth around that?" Tom asks. Mike answers him by taking an enormous bite. Only one pickle slice falls into the sand. He picks it up and considers eating it, then drops it into the trash sack. Everything they carry in has to be carried out.

"Are you wearing sunscreen?" Olivia pokes Mike's shoulder tentatively. "You're as red as the rock."

"He's wearing tanning solution," Tom says.

"That stuff doesn't keep you from burning," says Rob.

"Hell," says Mike. "My only souvenir—a tan, a burn. They won't let us take anything else out of the canyon."

"You got to eat the trout you caught," Allie says. She's a little sore that he didn't share.

"Yeah, I guess that's leaving the canyon in some form," says Mike. The groover bags are all stored somewhere beneath the deck.

Allie makes a face, raises her eyebrows at Elaine.

"After we eat, we hike up to the plaque," says Chip. He's told them about the men who separated from Powell's first expedition. "We'll get a group picture." He turns to Elaine. "You've never seen it."

She shakes her head. "This is new territory for us. *We* took out at Diamond Creek, ten-fifteen miles back. A little Indian bus took us back up to the top of the canyon."

"What I want to know," interrupts Vin, "is why those guys left Powell *here*."

"Yeah," says Allie. "I don't see any white water."

"Remember," Chip says, "Hoover Dam didn't go in until 1935. This here is really part of Lake Mead now. I guess Separation was the mother of all rapids before that. The guys who left Powell were sure the guys on the boat were going to die. And the guys on the boat were sure the guys who left them were going to die. Guys on the boat were right."

"Lotta guys on boats did die," says Allie. She has been reading a book Chip keeps in a locker—stories of those who met their end on the Colorado. She is especially impressed with the story of the honeymooners who drowned in 1928.

Elaine struggles, pole, step up, pole, step up, trying to follow Allie, who seems to be skipping up the side of the hill. Suddenly, she stops and turns around. "Hey, Elaine," she says. "I'll wait for you." The others, even Rob, are ahead. Elaine pants and grunts and hopes the sounds are taken as signs of appreciation.

Chip sets a camera on a rock. "Gather up," he says, and herds them against the wall next to the plaque. He pushes the button, then scurries back to the group. Mike and Rob make Vulcan salutes. "Grin," Chip says, "whether you feel like it or not." They all grin. Elaine feels like it.

"The irony," Chip says, "is that Powell's boat ran Separation with no trouble at all. The three guys got to the top of the canyon, but no further. Probably killed by Indians."

"Maybe they were translated," Rob says.

"Probably not to heaven," says Chip. "Maybe to hell. Isn't that what happens to quitters?"

Last night was hell. First that business with Olivia. When they settled onto their cots, and, for the first time all week, Elaine had gone to sleep immediately. Then she heard Rob's voice. "We've got to set up the tent, Elaine. It's starting to storm."

Chip appeared with the spotlight to help them. They could hear the others too, cussing. Theirs was such an old tent, smaller than those of the others—the tent that they had taken, new, down the Colorado decades before, the tent they hadn't used for years although they had set it up on the back patio to make sure it still worked, that they could still work it. They had to leave the cots behind, grabbing their pads and sleeping bags and their daypacks and pushing everything in. Inside they lay side by side, close together for the first time this trip, listening to the rain beating on the tent, the wind blowing.

"I'm not having much fun," Elaine had said.

Now, as they start back down the hill from the plaque, Elaine slips. Mike gets to her first, stands her up. "You okay?" Rob is in front of her, holding the tip of her pole. "Elaine?" he asks.

Her tailbone feels shattered, but she can stand. She closes her eyes for a second, then does what she always does. "I'm fine," she lies. "Let's go." She moves one foot ahead of the other, leaning heavily on her poles. My tailbone's jammed into my hip bone, she sings to herself. My hip bone's jammed into my thigh bone. What comes next? Oh hear the word of the Lord. Oh yes.

Day 9, Lake Mead

THE CHANNEL WIDENS AGAIN, AND HERE THEY ARE IN THE lake, about 300 river miles, Chip says, from their starting point. The canyon has flattened out—it is the desert of Elaine's childhood and adolescence, not a *grand* canyon, though the mountains in the distance look purplish and pretty. They camped near Pierce Ferry last night—their last night on the sand, and no, she certainly isn't sorry about that though Rob is whimpering about it all ending. One spot they just passed, Chip told them, is called God's Pocket.

Elaine likes that name. God's Pocket. This lake is the lake of her childhood too, and in those days she felt tucked safely in God's Pocket.

Her family didn't used to come to this part of the lake—they went to the other side on the flat beaches near the road to Boulder

City. Here the sand slopes onto the beach, and families have set up watered plastic chutes that children slide down. Elaine looks at them through the right side of her binoculars. When she was a child, they didn't take toys to the lake. There were anchored rafts, and you could swim to one, haul yourself up and sun a while, then get back in the cold water and swim to the next. Ben and Steve learned to swim before she did even though they were younger. They weren't afraid of the water and the muddy bottom of the lake the way she was. There were picnic tables, where families would bring potato salad and cold chicken and watermelon and cookies. Once she crawled underneath one of the picnic tables in a game of hide-and-seek, and she was bitten all over by a hill of red ants. She cried all the way home, and her mother ran a tub of tepid water and dumped in a box of baking soda for her sit in.

Mom. As hard as it has been for her and Rob to keep up, their load has been lighter because Ben and Bertie have been dealing with Mom.

And all the other things she hasn't given a thought to. No radio, no TV, no computers, no papers, none of those horrific articles that she herself could have written a couple of years ago. And the day-to-day sad images of life in L.A.—the homeless encampments under the freeway onramps, the men sifting through the recycling bins to fill shopping carts with aluminum cans, but mostly the scenes from the nursing home. The woman across the hall from Mom, the one who shrieks for hours on end.

How quiet it is here now that the river isn't surging through its prison walls. Chip has set up a canopy on the deck so they don't broil as they lunch on what's left in the cooler—some cheese, some crackers, some apples and oranges, a lot of Oreos, and cans of Mountain Dew, which, as Rob points out to Chip, has plenty of caffeine and an unconscionable amount of sugar. Chip shrugs.

"Bath time!" shouts Mike, who has stripped off his life jacket.

He holds up a plastic bottle and leaps into the lake. Vin and Allie shed their water sandals and life jackets and jump in next. Tom whispers something to Olivia, and in a minute they are bobbing up and down in the water too, Olivia giggling while Tom pours shampoo onto her head. Before Elaine can look over to Rob, she sees him descending the rope ladder that Chip has unwound.

"Go on, Aunt Elaine," says Chip. "I have to stay with the boat."

"I could stay with you," she says.

"Naw. Go on. You want to."

He's right—she does want to. It's the one thing she can do. She unzips the bottoms of her zip-off pants, undoes the lifejacket and sandals, and slides smoothly into the water. It feels glorious, warmer than the pool she uses at home, and, wonder of wonders, she doesn't hurt anywhere; she can move everything. She breast strokes, keeping her head above the water so she can see the others splashing, sudsing, tossing the shampoo bottle, squealing.

Rob paddles over to her, tugs on her shirt, smiles. She smiles back.

This afternoon, they will take the J-Rig out of the water at South Cove. Tomorrow they'll be back in the world of worry, but she pushes that out of her mind right now. Tomorrow worry. Today squint into the blue, blue sky and be buoyed up by the water, water that has rushed through the most sublime of all the ancient canyons, the grandest canyon of all.

Lauren,
Charlotte

Aunt Charlotte's Secrets

AUNT CHARLOTTE, COCOONED IN HER FLOWERED PIL-lows and comforter, looked out the bedroom window at the tulip magnolia tree. Curled beside her on the bed was a particularly scrawny cat named Jenny Craig, who had joined the household last fall, about the time it became clear that Aunt Charlotte was not going to get well. Uncle Baxter tolerated the family menagerie, paid the medical bills for the four feline strays, cleaned the cage of the cockatiels, but his heart belonged to Betsy, the black Lab he had inherited from his mother. Lauren wondered if afterwards he would keep the rest.

Sitting in the lotus position on a big cushion, Lauren stroked the white fur of the one decorative cat, Moby Mick. Occasionally Aunt Charlotte would look their way with a small smile. Mom said Aunt Charlotte had never been happy, never satisfied, always restless, reckless, but it seemed to Lauren that Aunt Charlotte didn't look as desolate as the circumstances warranted. Every Thursday she was frailer, but still she summoned small smiles. On Thursdays Lauren's last class ended at 2:00, and she took the train across the bay to the city and the Geary bus out to the flat on Tenth Avenue. She would stay till after supper—usually an omelet which she and Uncle Baxter assembled and shared—and he would drive her back to the Civic Center station.

Lauren unbuckled her sandals. It seemed right just to sit quietly and hum a little and pet the closest cat. Sometimes Aunt Charlotte uttered epigrams that Lauren would record later in her journal, like "Pain makes us pay attention," and "Even an orchid withers." That was what she said last week when she was showing Lauren the scar from the November surgery, the one they didn't bother to complete. There were other scars. The one running like a zipper up her calf recalled a fall from a motorcycle in Genoa the summer she was 21. The thin red line that ridged her left eyebrow and disappeared into the hair on her temple she got clambering up Half Dome with a man named Jackson. "And then there are the scars you can't see," Aunt Charlotte said.

Sometimes Aunt Charlotte asked questions, mostly ludicrous questions like "What would you do if your Martin joined the Marines?" or "How would you feel if your mother stopped nagging everyone to go to church?" Now, as Lauren drifted into a daydream in which Martin was untypically tender, in which he actually *touched* her, Aunt Charlotte's voice punctured the reverie. "Are you happy, dear?" There was always a kind of catch in Aunt Charlotte's voice. Lauren put the dream on hold. Was she happy? She must not be or the word "yes" would have burst from her mouth. But she wasn't miserable either. Maybe she was like Aunt Charlotte. "I'm okay," she said after a while. Aunt Charlotte looked at her, a long look, and then turned back to the window so that Lauren could see the dusky red braid that Uncle Baxter must have twisted this morning and bound with a lavender ribbon. The braid was short and stubby. It was the only substantial part of Aunt Charlotte's body.

The hospice nurse came every morning now and measured the morphine, and Uncle Baxter, who was on family leave from the FAA, patrolled the flat in his red suspenders and plaid pants. He kept the furniture dusted and the dishes washed up in between the Friday visits of the cleaning lady. The cleaning lady was a male drama student named Kyle who used a lawn rake on the carpet in the living room. After their Thursday supper, Lauren and Uncle Baxter would stomp around in the living room to flatten down the carpet so that Kyle would have something to do.

"You were a gorgeous baby," Aunt Charlotte said suddenly. Her hollow face looked saintly, ethereal in the late-afternoon light. "Curly black hair, long eyelashes."

Lauren leaned back against the armoire. "My hair's only curly when it's very short." She tugged her bangs down to the tops of her eyebrows. "Like now."

"We used to call that a pixie cut. You always looked like a little pixie. Back then I thought I'd probably have little pixies of my own." She stroked a little circle between Jenny Craig's ears.

Why didn't you, Lauren wanted to ask, but she rubbed a little circle between Moby Mick's ears instead.

"Open the third drawer there." Aunt Charlotte motioned with her head towards the big dresser. "On the right."

Lauren dumped Moby, pushed herself up, and pulled open the drawer. Bright scarves were stacked in neat, soft piles. Mom said that Aunt Charlotte had been a terrible housekeeper until she got sick. Then she set about putting everything in order. "Everything but her spiritual affairs," Mom had said and had cleared her throat for emphasis.

Aunt Charlotte cleared her throat too. "There's a box at the bottom. In the back." Lauren found it and lifted it up. Aunt Charlotte nodded. "Open it."

Lauren unfolded two little crocheted dresses, one peach with black ribbon, one pearl white. "Those were yours," Aunt Charlotte said. "I made them for you. Your mother gave them back to me, in case I had my own daughter. I want you to have them. Maybe some day you'll have a little girl."

Lauren laid the dresses out on the comforter. "Oh Aunt Charlotte," she said.

"But even if you don't have children, you should have them." She breathed out. "They probably aren't fashionable any more. Even babies have to be fashionable now."

"I want them," Lauren said. "Thank you." She sat on the bed and fingered the white dress. "I didn't know you could make things like this. I never saw you crochet." She couldn't picture Aunt Charlotte sitting on the sofa doing needlework in front of the television like her mother. Before the cancer, if the television in the den was on, Aunt Charlotte would be stretched out on the carpet, pumping an imaginary bicycle in the air and scowling at Uncle Baxter, slouched in his reclining chair.

"I haven't done handwork in years. But when you were little, I even sewed. I liked making you things. Once I made you a green dragon. And when you were first born, I pieced a crib quilt out of your grandmother's old cotton scraps. You dragged the quilt everywhere, wore it right out. I don't know what happened to the dragon."

"Maybe Nita got it."

"Maybe."

Lauren felt brave. "Did you—want to have children?"

Aunt Charlotte didn't answer for so long that Lauren thought maybe she hadn't heard. Finally she said, "Sometimes. If I'd been able to believe in something, then maybe. Or if I'd been able to believe in nothing at all."

Lauren waited but no more words came. "And Uncle Baxter?"

Aunt Charlotte paused again. "Either way was okay with him." She reached for the peach dress. "I don't see this color much nowadays."

"No," Lauren said. "But it's very pretty."

Betsy wandered into the bedroom, put her paws up on Lauren's jeans, tongued her chin. Lauren fended the Lab off with her elbows. "Baxter!" Aunt Charlotte called. For good measure she buzzed her intercom button. "Baxter, come get this dog!"

When Uncle Baxter peered into the room, Betsy abandoned Lauren, bounded to Uncle Baxter and licked his hands. "Come on girl," he said, ushering Betsy out the door. "We know when we're not wanted." Lauren gave a half wave.

"I heard a great dog story yesterday," she offered. "From my math teacher. He had a turkey, a pet turkey, I think, anyway they weren't going to eat it. . . ." She looked at Aunt Charlotte, who was stroking the peach dress. "Last summer when they were going on a long vacation, they took the turkey up to his dad's farm in Marin County. His dad had a Rottweiler pup." Aunt

Charlotte winced, maybe from the pain, maybe for the turkey. "When my teacher got back from his trip, he went to his dad's place. His dad said, 'I'm sorry. You can't have the turkey back. The Rottweiler, well—' And my teacher thought, oh no, even a baby Rottweiler can probably, well, knock the stuffing out of a turkey, but his father took them around to the back to see. The Rottweiler pup and the turkey had bonded. The pup followed the turkey everywhere."

Aunt Charlotte sighed in relief, then gave a short laugh. "Bonding's a big thing nowadays. When I was young, we didn't use that word. When a woman had a baby . . ." She smiled as if she were looking at something inside her, then shook her head and brought herself back to the bedroom. "I'm always reading about bonding now. Women ask for maternity leave so they can bond with their babies. They don't say they want to *be* with their babies—they want to *bond* with them."

"I don't feel bonded now with Mom," Lauren said. "My friend Sarah—she's in the dorm, across the hall—she claims that's normal. It's always so complicated, the feelings you have about your mother."

"Maybe that's what bonding means. Developing complicated feelings."

"Well, if that's so," said Lauren, "it's overrated." She reached for her backpack and carefully put the two little dresses on top of her calculus book. "I feel more bonded with you than with Mom."

"That's a different kind of bonding. You mean 'comfortable with.'"

"True," Lauren said. "You worry about me just the right amount. And you don't worry about my 'eternal salvation.'" She turned to look at Aunt Charlotte. "Do you?"

Aunt Charlotte laughed.

"And you don't feel any guilt about me," Lauren continued, "and I don't feel any guilt about you. Women shouldn't have daughters. They should have nieces."

"I dropped you once." Aunt Charlotte lifted her hand to her forehead as if she were taking her own temperature, then flinched and closed her eyes before starting again to pet Jenny Craig. "That made me feel guilty."

"I must have recovered."

"Maybe we did bond," Aunt Charlotte said gently. "The first three months of your life, I spent more time with you than Ramona did."

Lauren stood up. "What do you mean?" She rounded the bed and scrunched up cross-legged on Uncle Baxter's pillow.

Aunt Charlotte didn't turn her head. "Your mom kind of freaked out. Now it's called postpartum depression, but we didn't know much about it then. She closed herself up in the bedroom and wouldn't come out. She didn't have enough milk for you anyway, so you were already on formula. Didn't seem to have hurt you any."

Lauren bent closer to Aunt Charlotte. "So you took care of me?"

"Your dad phoned, all upset. It was the first week of June. I had a summer job lined up. I called and told them I had a family emergency. I moved in with the three of you, into that tiny apartment in Culver City. I slept on the couch. By the start of fall semester, Ramona was pretty much okay."

"Mom never told me that."

Aunt Charlotte drew her lips in. "No. Better to not mention it to her, I think. It's nothing to be ashamed of, but she's not proud of it. I'm pretty sure she never told any of her church people. She let them think she had physical complications."

"She did okay after Nita was born?"

Aunt Charlotte grimaced. "Not really okay. But better. Only about six weeks. I was in St. Louis, and I couldn't come, so your grandma took care of Nita and you."

"So it was Grandma who bonded with Nita," Lauren said. There were so many puzzles. She thought back to when Grandma died. Nita *had* been inconsolable. "So was Nita a formula-fed baby too?"

"I expect so," Aunt Charlotte said. She leaned towards her nightstand and grasped her water glass. "What will you do," she asked, as if they had been talking about it all along, "with a degree in biology?"

"If I *get* a degree," Lauren said. "I don't even get to start taking classes in my major till the fall. Maybe I won't like it."

"You'll get a degree," said Aunt Charlotte, "in biology or something else. Do you want to teach?"

"I don't know. Did you know from the start you wanted to be a dietitian?"

"I didn't really want to be a dietitian. But my cousin Melba was a dietitian and she could always get work and it wasn't bad work. It left her time to play."

"What did you *want* to be?"

Aunt Charlotte shrugged. "A folk singer."

"Really?"

"Most of us cloistered little girls in the youth choir wanted to be folk singers." She pushed herself up a few inches higher, and her eyes gleamed. "I had a bedroom to myself when Ramona got married, and I would swirl around the bed clutching a make-believe microphone and shout out the lyrics to the songs on my radio."

"Did you have a guitar?"

"I did. I could empty the house with 'Go Tell Aunt Rhody'! And I grew my hair long and straight like Joan Baez. Your grandma was appalled."

Lauren laughed. "Joan Baez looks so—well, respectable."

Aunt Charlotte nodded. "She does now, doesn't she?"

"What *I* really want to do," said Lauren, "is study bird migration. And I want to go to Antarctica."

Aunt Charlotte whistled. "*I* wanted to go to Paris. Antarctica!" Her veiny hands smoothed Jenny Craig's fur.

"And New Zealand," said Lauren. "Are you sorry now you were a dietitian?" She hadn't meant to use the past tense.

Aunt Charlotte didn't seem to notice. "No. It was my job, but it wasn't my life."

"Maybe I'll go into the Peace Corps," Lauren said. "My math teacher was in the Peace Corps. He went to Sri Lanka."

"*I* planned to go into the Peace Corps," Aunt Charlotte said. "I filled out the forms. I talked to people." Her voice suddenly became limp. "I—couldn't pass the physical. I got a job in St. Louis. And then I met Baxter. Two sheep who'd lost the way." She said it in almost a whisper, then cleared her throat and found her voice again. "Could you eat a chocolate chip cookie? Someone brought us a big plateful, and I can't eat them. You can afford the calories better than Baxter can."

Lauren slid off the bed and headed towards the kitchen. "I think he put them in the breadbox," Aunt Charlotte called, and Lauren found them there. There were crumbs on the cabinet top and a few ants. She wet a paper towel and squashed them. Martin would not approve, but Martin was in the anatomy lab, not here. She made a small stack of cookies, poured herself a glass of orange juice, and carried it all back to the bedroom.

"Would you like anything?" she asked.

Aunt Charlotte shook her head. "All those years working with food—and food's the last thing I want to see."

"Orange juice though? Something cool to drink?"

"Water. Room temperature water." Aunt Charlotte gestured towards her nightstand where a glass with a straw sat atop one of Grandma's doilies. "That's all that tastes good to me."

"Yummy cookies." Lauren held up the remnant of one. "Who made them?" She sat again on Uncle Baxter's pillow.

"Maggie, downstairs. I think she's scheming to snare Baxter when I'm gone." She laughed as if she only cared a little. "One day," she said, "I was at a patient's bedside, it was when I worked at the convalescent home in Daly City, and there was a bag of cookies there. I was thinking that I would like to try one when the patient, he was an old man, said *he*'d like to try one. His granddaughter had made them. 'But I need my teeth,' he said. He pointed to a margarine container and there was half a set of false teeth." She paused. "Have you ever even seen false teeth?"

Lauren shook her head.

"Well, imagine a row of teeth set in pink plastic. The man had his own teeth on the top and these were for the bottom, but I didn't really know what to do with them. I put them in upside down." She chortled. "Finally I got it figured out. I keep seeing his face, his eyes so big, knowing something was wrong, but not sure what!"

"Did he offer you a cookie?"

"No. And the next day he died."

"Oh."

"Death isn't the scariest thing," Aunt Charlotte said after a moment, "in case you were wondering."

Lauren settled herself sideways so she could look at Aunt Charlotte. Moby leapt up on the bed and pushed his forehead against Lauren's hand until she began to stroke him. What *was* the scariest thing? What was scarier than dropping off the edge of the world into nothing? But she waited too long to ask, and Aunt Charlotte's eyelids lowered and her mouth sagged open and she coasted into sleep. Lauren watched her for a few minutes to make sure she was breathing okay, and then she deposited Moby on Uncle Baxter's pillow, retrieved her orange juice glass, and padded down the hall.

In the kitchen, black ants were swarming on the floor, radiating out from Betsy's food bowl. Uncle Baxter was in his study, at his computer, so Lauren looked under the sink and found a plastic spray can of Raid. It wasn't at all ecological to spray poison on ants, but she couldn't carry them outside one by one the way she did spiders. She hesitated. In the broom closet, she found the Dustbuster, and she plugged it in and sucked some of them up. Routed, the circle spread.

Uncle Baxter appeared at the kitchen door.

"Ants," she said.

"Here," he said. "Just spray." He put Betsy's bowl in the sink and ran water into it, then took the Raid can and aimed at the now frantic army of ants. "Open the window." He gave the Dustbuster a squirt too.

The two of them retreated, gasping, into the living room. Uncle Baxter pushed a side window open. The air was cool outside, but they stood there breathing it in.

"Martin has become a vegetarian," Lauren said.

Uncle Baxter grunted. "Why would he do a thing like that?"

"He talks about the sanctity of life. Even insect life."

"I don't eat insects myself," said Uncle Baxter.

Lauren elbowed him. "I hate to kill them. They must be as aware of things as Betsy is. When they see a thumb coming at them, or a spray can, they must be afraid. We read a George Orwell essay in English about a man who was hanged in Burma. On the way to the gallows he walked around a puddle of water. It was such a normal, human thing to do. It made Orwell feel terrible."

Uncle Baxter grunted again, in a not very convinced way.

"Ants walk around puddles too," she said.

"All that proves," Uncle Baxter said, "is that walking around puddles is *not* a normal, human thing to do. And anyway, think about the life of an ant. No books, no music, probably not even any nieces." He winked. "Just work, work, work. Maybe for ants, the end isn't such a terrible thing."

Lauren looked down at the street below. "For humans it is terrible." She let her voice lift up a little at the end.

"Sometimes it's a blessed rest."

"Is Aunt Charlotte afraid?"

He rubbed his hands. He wore a heavy gold band on his left ring finger. "I hope not."

"I'd be afraid."

"You're young. And you don't hurt."

She shivered a little. "Does Aunt Charlotte believe there's something after?"

"I don't think she's counting on it."

"Do you think there is?"

"I don't know." The oldest of the cats, Susie, poked her head between his legs. He patted her briefly, then straightened up. "I'm afraid not."

"Would you like there to be?"

He sighed. "If it could be a good place. A place with no cancer." He smiled. "And no arthritis. And if there were a separate place for ants and mosquitoes and people who think they're better than everyone else." He shut the window. "Let's stomp down the carpet," he said, "since we're in here."

The buzzer sounded in his study.

"I'll go," Lauren said. "I'll see what she wants."

They both went. Aunt Charlotte was almost sitting up. Her eyes looked a little wild, and she was breathing hard. "My mother was here," she said. Lauren and Uncle Baxter looked quickly at each other. "She was standing right there," Aunt Charlotte said, "where you're standing."

"Char," said Uncle Baxter, moving closer. He took her right hand and rocked it.

"What did she do?" Lauren asked. "What did Grandma do?"

"I think she was singing hymns. One of those old hymns. I could see her. I know you don't believe me, but I could see her."

"She was just singing?" asked Lauren. "Did she say anything? What did she look like? Did she look the way she did when she was old?"

"I don't know," Aunt Charlotte said. "I just know it was my mother. Singing. Betsy stopped her. That Betsy came into the room, and Mother left."

"Your mother never did like dogs," said Uncle Baxter.

Aunt Charlotte closed her eyes.

Lauren knelt on the bed and took Aunt Charlotte's left hand. "Do you want us to stay here? Do you want anything?"

Aunt Charlotte relaxed and lay back. "No, dear." Her eyes were still closed. "Just sleep." She motioned with her chin to the bolster behind her, and Uncle Baxter slipped the bolster off the bed and settled Aunt Charlotte's head on her pillow.

"It's the morphine," Uncle Baxter said as Lauren chopped mushrooms and onions and red bell peppers.

"I'm glad though," she said. "It's probably easier if you think there's someone there to, you know, show you the way." She scooted the vegetables into the sauté pan and nudged Betsy aside. "I'd like for Aunt Charlotte to show *me* the way."

"When I was a child," he said, "five or six, I used to pray that I would die at the same moment as my mother. I knew how dreadfully I would miss her and I somehow also knew that if I died first, she would suffer unspeakable sorrow. When I got older, I understood that I could bear her death better than she could bear mine. That's what happened, of course. She's been gone seven years now." He stirred the vegetables while Lauren grated cheese. "I love Charlotte. It's easy to still love Charlotte. She hasn't become someone else. She's the same cranky, the same sorry afterwards." He laughed, then stopped abruptly. "I don't have to try and remember the person I used to care for—she's still that person. But now if I could pray, I'd pray that she would die peacefully and soon. And I'm not ready to go yet."

Lauren slipped Betsy a little piece of cheddar. "Is Aunt Charlotte ready?"

He sighed. "I don't know. She's almost ready, I think."

"You used to pray, huh?"

"When I was a child," he said. "Your mother still prays. She writes us how she's praying morning, noon, and night for us. She doesn't say what say what she's asking for."

"That's Mom," Lauren said, pouring the eggs into the bigger pan. "She prays for me too. I guess I should be glad. In case there *is* anything, she's covering my ass."

Uncle Baxter grinned. "I'd like to think it did some good. But then I remember all those people who die in earthquakes and plane crashes and wars, and I just know that some of them were praying. And why listen to me if he didn't listen to them?"

Lauren divided and slid the omelet onto plates and set them on the table. Uncle Baxter poured seltzer water into goblets. He lifted his glass. "To Charlotte," he said.

"To Charlotte." Lauren touched her glass to his.

Betsy settled herself underneath the table, his paws on Lauren's bare feet. "Another fine omelet," Uncle Baxter said. "Does Martin eat eggs?"

"This week."

"Bring him over." He shrugged with his hands. "When all this is finished."

AFTER SUPPER, THEY LOOKED IN ON AUNT CHARLOTTE. She was mumbling in her sleep, so Uncle Baxter pulled over the needle-pointed stool and sat next to her as she slept. "I'll clean up," Lauren said. "Are you sure you want to leave her to take me downtown?"

"I'll call Maggie, downstairs," he said. "She'll drive you."

Instead of rinsing the dishes and arranging them in the dishwasher, Lauren filled the sink. It was satisfying to wash dishes. The dorm denied her that simple task. Her arms were cool—the kitchen window was still open—and the hot water felt good. Betsy wandered in again and nuzzled her leg, so she crouched down and poured kibble into the now clean dog bowl. What was that sound? She knelt, motionless, and listened. In their bedroom, Uncle Baxter was singing. "Abide with me," he sang, "fast falls the eventide. La la la la la la la la la la." A hymn he hadn't quite forgotten. It was comforting. He even sounded comforted. Resigned. It had something to do with no longer having hope.

Lauren had hope. She didn't have faith maybe, the faith of her mother, of her father—but she had hope. She straightened up and stretched. The smell of the insecticide lingered. There on the window sill were a few confused-looking ants. She waited till they marched close together, then gently blew them out into the night.

Requiem in L Minor

I N THE OLD ADDRESS BOOK, THE L PAGES ARE IMPOS-
sible—street numbers lined out, zip codes scratched in, whole
entries x'd or margined with a question mark. Even the H's are
more decipherable. Now, on the dining room table, the new
address book is lying open waiting for me to carry on. To mark
my place I stick the ragged Post-it that Baxter had affixed to the
cover five years ago: "Dearest Char, the rest of this present is
my offer to copy and correct all entries in legible handwriting."
The new book, the cover awash with birds, was a Valentine's gift.
Baxter never got around to giving me the rest of the present.

Baxter was awash in good intentions. Now he is just awash—
aimlessly floating, fighting the flow. Sometimes he is all affection.
Sometimes he can hardly look at me. Eighteen years, mostly
good. More than a partnership, our tiny family. No parents, no
children, but Lauren is coming over this afternoon, after her
classes. She comes every week now. I know it's her idea, not
Ramona's though I imagine she reports on me to her mother. If
Lauren were my daughter, instead of my niece, she'd probably
feel she *had* to be here. Instead she's relaxed, doesn't say much,
just plops down on the floor or on my bed. A gift in a kid who's
not even twenty.

Ramona drove up once after the diagnosis. She couldn't sit for
more than a minute. She walked back and forth, from Cocky's
cage to the window. She kept asking if she could do anything,
laundry, vacuuming. I told her we have a husky housecleaner,
Kyle, but she seemed not to hear. Two, maybe three times this
year, she's phoned, but she can't think of anything to say or

maybe she can't make herself say what she is thinking. Instead she mails us notes, lots of notes, on flowered cards, and tells us she is praying for us.

Ever since I started college and stopped church, ever since I let loose of that iron rod and the word of God, she has felt threatened by me, has disapproved of me. Of me and my men, she would say. But sisters share so much. I know she will be distraught when I die.

I chew the top of my pen. It tastes about as good as the mush Baxter brings me for breakfast. Everything tastes bitter. Today is a good day though, just a little dizziness. Moby brushes against my leg, waits for me to massage his neck, then bounds onto my lap and stretches up to the table. He's taken a liking to the big wooden bowl in the center, and he curls up now inside it. The bowl was a gift from Nathan, when we were young in Berkeley, two decades ago. I shake my head, rattle and rearrange my thoughts. I have spent the last months stacking and sorting. Now I am redoing the address book, myself, struggling to make my letters legible so that Baxter will be able to find everyone. Well, almost everyone.

Angela and Mark Laird

I WAS MAID OF HONOR WHEN MARK AND ANGIE GOT MARried. I was seventeen, two years younger than Angela and the other bridesmaids, all of us stuffed into red velvet dresses and red suede pumps. I didn't go to the actual wedding because it was in the Mormon temple, where you had to do special things and make special promises. Everyone assumed that some day I would have a temple wedding, too; no one was disappointed in me yet. I stood next to Angie during the reception because we were second cousins whose mothers were not just cousins— they were best friends who had long hoped that their daughters, Angela and Charlotte, would become best friends too.

We never did. I adored Angie's mom. Vilate was lively and funny and quick; Angie was lethargic and simple and slow. When my folks left me at Vilate's house in Palmdale for a week every summer, I was scrunched into a three-quarters bed with Angie, who slept very soundly and took up more than her share of the space. I wasn't used to bumping into someone else's arms and legs at night. Even the years Ramona and I had to share a bedroom, she had the upper bunk because she was so much older, and I had the lower bunk to myself.

Except for the nights, though, I liked going to Palmdale. Angie and I played croquet next door, in her uncle's big backyard, with more cousins, including the handsome Lewis, who bragged that he would join the Army when he was eighteen. We tromped downtown to the little grocery store Angie's dad managed, and he gave us Tootsie Rolls and Necco wafers. We hung out with Angie's friend Bonnie Alice, across the street, and looked through movie magazines.

And then suddenly Angie was nineteen, and her roundness became almost voluptuous, and her white-blonde hair was smooth and fine. She surprised everyone by making it through a year of college and met, through her handsome cousin Lewis, Mark, an almost-as-handsome second lieutenant in the army. They were married just before Christmas. When they moved to Texas, Angie sent me recipes for Marshmallow Jello Cool Whip mousse and German chocolate cake. I was taking a college English course, and I knew that my teacher would have scrawled all over Angie's letters with a red marking pen.

Angie and Mark visited Palmdale every summer, and they'd drive over to La Crescenta to see us while I was still living at home. Every summer Angie looked fatter. After half a dozen miscarriages, she finally carried a baby to term, but he died in the hospital, and she almost died too. Though Mark's faith wobbled, every loss somehow reaffirmed Angie's. Through the church welfare services, they adopted two boys, who, according to Mom in later years, didn't turn out so well, by which she probably meant that they didn't turn out to be bookies or burglars, but they didn't turn out to be Mormon either.

When Vilate died of stomach cancer, Mom felt she had inherited the responsibility to lecture Angie on her weight. "You don't want to lose that handsome husband of yours," she would say. Angie would giggle and agree, but, after all, Mark was a loyal, church-going, tithe-paying Scoutmaster, a little too stout to turn many heads, and about as likely to stray as a turnip. At her dad's funeral, I noticed that Angie panted a lot. She waddled rather than walked. A few weeks after she buried her father, Angie died too, of a heart attack, and Mark remarried a year after that and moved to Florida, where the more promising of their boys works in a repair shop for golf carts.

In the old book, I trace a light line through Angie and Mark's address and phone number. Was Angie mostly happy in her life? Did her disappointments force her to reexamine her obedience, her passivity, her beliefs?

I hope not. I hope Angie did what I couldn't do. I hope she kept the faith.

Nathan Loewe

AT LEAST I KNOW WHERE ANGIE IS. MORE OR LESS. MARK had her body buried in Palmdale, next to her folks. Now Nathan— Nathan and I were born the very same night. Once we figured out that we were born the very same hour—he in Cleveland, I in Burbank. We met when we were twenty-two—I lived in the apartment directly beneath his in the twelve-unit building close to Cal, where he was a senior architecture student, and close to the hospital, where I was a dietetic intern. Nathan didn't have much hair, but he had class and confidence. I had lots of hair—it exploded around my face and down my back when I took off the net I had to wear at work—but I felt a little inferior in Berkeley because I had majored at a small state college in what was then called "food science."

That year, Nathan and I spent countless hours together. We stomped our feet and clapped our hands for the banjo players at the Freight and Salvage. We walked the neighborhoods at night, covertly culling flowers from front yards. We talked about his inconvenient Jewish heritage and my inconvenient Mormon one and our roommates (who were briefly in love with each other) and studies and work and so many things, but I wonder now—has he had a lover of any sort? Was he gay? I am shocked that I don't know.

I do know crazy things about Nathan—like his being the executor of the will of his elderly, eccentric aunt, who lived in Chicago. The aunt always told Nathan that she didn't trust banks and their safety deposit boxes, so when she was gone, he should search for her valuables in her apartment—like hundred-dollar bills between the dinner plates and diamond rings in tubs of margarine in the refrigerator. When she died, he dutifully went to Chicago and ferreted about the kitchen. There were many partially used tubs of margarine in the refrigerator. Not one was the repository for jewels. There were many sets of china in the cupboards. There was no money hidden between the dishes. Nathan grumbled every time he stuck his finger into margarine, every time he unstacked his aunt's dinnerware.

Until I met Morty, Nathan and I celebrated our birthday together. We exchanged presents—his, always something beautiful—a glass music box, a polished serving tray, that big wooden bowl now full of big white cat. Once Nathan cooked the two of us a birthday dinner in his new flat in the city. Once I cooked. Once we made reservations a month ahead for Chez Panisse. Even after Morty, even after I went off to St. Louis and married Baxter and after we moved to San Francisco ourselves, Nathan and I still called each other on our birthday. At least once he came to dinner at the flat on Chenery Street. I can't remember exactly when I lost him, when a funny birthday card I mailed him was returned. I couldn't find him in phone books. I couldn't find him on the internet. If he *were* gay—well, lots of gays have disappeared in San Francisco.

There's a cube of butter, but no tubs of margarine in our refrigerator. And there is only dust between the plates.

What if—most apt and awful of happenstances—Nathan and I are to die on the same day? And unless some sort of spirit whispers such secrets, neither of us will know.

Carole and Ken Lidwell

CAROLE MAY STILL BE AROUND SOMEWHERE, MAYBE EVEN on the next block. One can hide in cities though she wasn't the hiding kind. Carole doesn't have the same phone, but she may have the same name, the same husband, the same address. Somehow, however, I don't think so.

We four used to do things together, subscribed to the same symphony series, usually met for dinner first. Though we were both fond of Carole, Baxter didn't like Ken, said he was "rigid as a robot." I didn't like him either. Ken was Carole's third husband. When I first met her, in a yoga class at the Unitarian Church, we discovered we had both been Mormons once upon a time. The past seemed to weigh less heavily on Carole though. She was good at getting rid of things—sixty pounds, long hair, gray hair, two husbands, three sisters who had unacceptably right-wing views on everything from abortion to Zionism. Like me, Carole had cats instead of children. Unlike me, she had an executive job with an insurance company and dressed like one of those women in the full-page newspaper ads—tailored pantsuits, silk blouses, discreet gold earrings.

One spring, Carole said Ken didn't want to renew the symphony subscription, but maybe she'd find someone else to make up the foursome, a woman friend. But she didn't. We exchanged Christmas greetings for a few years. Our Christmas card was always a picture of us surrounded by our feathered and furry menagerie, and Carole and Ken's was always a fancy gold-embossed card with curlicues and just their signatures. Then they didn't send a card at all for a few years, so we stopped sending them one too.

Where have they gone? Carole and Ken and Nathan. Surely not to graveyards every one. And what does the song mean, "long time passing"?

Jill Leonard

JILL'S MOM GLORIA WAS A LONG TIME PASSING. GLORIA was my all-time favorite resident in the Autumn Gardens Nursing Home where I worked until I couldn't. I didn't get to know all the residents as well as I knew Gloria, and I knew only a few of their children as well as I knew Jill. Gloria's face was twisted into a kind of grimace—not a stroke, she said when I first talked with her about her dietary preferences, but a failed operation to remove a tumor below her ear. Although she would get confused about time and place, Gloria was pretty sharp compared to most of the residents, and she could still walk those first years. She used a walker, one of those sit-down kinds, on which she kept her clipboard and crossword puzzles. "I'm a tough old bird," she boasted. During World War II, she had worked in the Richmond shipyards, "like Rosie the Riveter," she said.

Jill used to sneak through the side door of the kitchen to chat with me in my office behind the massive refrigerator. There were big black lines painted on the floor—beyond which only staff persons were supposed to go. Jill didn't visit her mother as often as she thought she should, and to my amateur-analyst eyes, she was a classic study in mother-daughter guilt. Jill wasn't an amateur—she was a psychologist, and she knew lots about guilt. She flew around the country, giving papers and listening to other people give papers. She had a lesbian partner with MS and an adult son with no job and a pregnant girlfriend.

My parents—but not my own guilt—gone, I paid a lot of attention to Gloria, giving her hand and shoulder squeezes and kisses on her powdery cheeks. Gloria was so different from my mom, who had crumpled into a little pile in her kitchen, cerebral hemorrhage they said, and died in a zippered blue housedress. Gloria went through periods of pulling her pant legs high above her knees. "I've always had good legs," she said. She didn't have bad legs, especially for a lady in a nursing home, but they were very white, and I always wanted to look away when she was in exhibition mode.

The average stay at Autumn Gardens was two years, but Gloria had over four years before she had to trade the walker for a wheelchair. Unlike some of the residents, she wasn't occupied with dying. She attended every activity the nursing home had to offer—word games, sing-a-longs, drumming, flower arranging. She went to Shabbat services with Rabbi Marsha on Friday evening, ecumenical Christian services with Reverend Pat on Sunday afternoon. "And I'm not even religious," she said. "What are *you*?" she asked me. I told her that I didn't go to any church, but Mormon hymns kept running through my head. When I sang her the first verse of "Come, Come, Ye Saints," she squealed with pleasure. Whenever we were more or less alone, Gloria would say, "C'mon, Charlotte. Belt out one of those Mormon ditties." And I would. Some things you can never forget.

And then Gloria stopped wheeling herself about the way the livelier residents did—using their feet and pulling themselves with the side rails in the halls. Some of the light dimmed in her eyes. She seemed depressed. "I'm not good for anything," she would say. I reassured her she was good for *me*. Jill became frantic, and I had to reassure her too, which wasn't easy because I knew what came next short term and, unlike my sister, have never known what came next long term. Gloria slept more and ate less. She liked sweets, so I ordered sweet sauces on everything that wasn't already dessert. She still paid attention to her appearance though—bright pink and red jackets and knit pants and big baubly jewelry. And she still sometimes showed off her white legs.

"It's *not* your fault," I told Jill who knew it wasn't her fault, but felt guilty anyway. I didn't tell Jill about my diagnosis.

When Gloria died, Jill and I promised to stay in touch, and I printed Jill's phone number neatly in the book. We didn't stay in touch though, and then I got really sick, and I couldn't imagine Jill would be happy to hear from me. I wouldn't have been happy to hear from me.

Morty Lawler

10 LOCKSLEY AVENUE. THAT'S STILL RIGHT. THE PHONE number too, probably. I know because—though I've not had contact with Morty for some years now, one of his ex-sisters-in-law has kept me apprised of his career and marriage changes. He's an agent for artists, artists who work with metals and sell iron banisters and house and garden sculptures to people who have a lot of money. Morty has always known people who had a lot of money. When I knew him well—or thought I did—he worked for Clorox, which paid him handsomely, but didn't suit his image of himself.

I was the woman after his first wife and before his second. I didn't last as long as either of them, but I apparently lasted longer than the third. He has children by the second, teenagers, a boy and a girl, whom he takes skiing and surfing, according to the ex-sister-in-law, who is very critical of his parenting skills. I think he's given up on marriage, but there is another woman in his life, one much younger, I think, an artist.

I was ecstatic the first year Morty and I were together. We biked all over Berkeley and backpacked in the Sierra and went to black churches in Oakland because the music was so fine. Then he took the job in the Midwest and suggested I come too and it all fell apart. I couldn't understand why. When he moved back to California, I stayed in St. Louis, too paralyzed to make any more changes. And then I met Baxter and returned to the world of the living. I mattered to Baxter. And he has a wonderfully long attention span.

We've seen Morty a few times over the years—run into him at a concert, a museum, once even at the funeral of a friend's father. The meetings weren't painful. He's gained a little weight and lost a lot of hair. Not from chemo either.

I'm not up to analyzing why I've kept Morty's contact info over the years, but this is a good time to divest myself of it. I make three straight lines through his name and two through his phone number and address. Ginny would approve.

Ginny Lin

AH, GINNY. I NEVER WROTE GINNY'S ENTRIES IN PEN, EVEN when I had recent addresses for her. Ginny had had so many addresses. In the old days, it seemed she would send a card every November with a new address to alert people with Christmas-card lists. She never included a letter, just a note ("Love hearing from you, girl!"), usually a picture. Usually a picture with a man, a different man from the year before. The last time I heard from her, Ginny had sent a picture of herself with *two* men, one black, one white. That one was from Chicago. Other cards had come from Atlanta and Boston, and a bunch had come from New York—all with different Manhattan or Brooklyn addresses. Baxter looked forward to Ginny's cards. He'd assign whimsical occupations to the assorted men. "That one probably sharpens knives at street fairs," he'd say. Or "Now she's gone and found a Latvian yoga coach."

Ginny and I had gone through college together, quitting for a couple of quarters to work and get enough money to ride a motorcycle around western Europe. Ginny did the driving; I straddled the rear seat. Back home, we introduced each other to unlikely men. Mom and Ramona had not approved of Ginny.

She was too exotic, too wild, too much fun. Too foreign, they thought, but didn't say, even though Ginny's grandparents had come to California before my parents had. When I was in big trouble, it was Ginny I could go to, Ginny who knew who would help.

That has been so long ago. After Baxter and I moved here, she would come visit us, stay a weekend, always coming in very late. We haven't heard from her now for five or six years, and the Christmas letters we have sent were returned stamped with a smeary "Not known at this address." But Ginny is around somewhere. She has too much energy to die. She's probably attached to the King of Bahrain or someone like that. She'll resurface eventually.

But probably not in time. Anyway, I no longer have the kind of problems Ginny can solve.

EVEN THE NEW ADDRESS BOOK LOOKS OLD. IT IS RATHER quaint. Kids like Lauren have probably never kept address books. They just store information on their computers and phones. Once there were rolodexes. Baxter used to have a box with business cards that he would occasionally alphabetize.

I was brought up to believe that there was a God with a really big address book. He kept track of everyone. That wasn't the metaphor used in Sunday School, but that was the idea. Mom and Ramona and maybe Dad accepted that idea. Ramona's girls, Lauren and Nita, don't appear to be believers though, which must cause Ramona more sorrow and shame than a wayward little sister ever could.

I close the old book and trace, with my finger, the birds on the cover of the new. I can't remember ever really believing in the devil—the way I never really believed in the Easter Bunny. Santa, now Santa I had believed in till Ramona shrieked out the truth in an argument when I was six. And Noah and Moses and Jesus, I believed their stories—though Jonah seemed pretty suspect even then. I tried, though, for years, on and off. Until there got to be too many troubles, too many transgressions, I tried.

"She's studying for finals," we used to say about someone who would "get 'ligion" at the nursing home. Not like Gloria. Gloria simply went to every activity at Autumn Gardens; if there had been an atheists' meeting, she would have attended that too.

But I wouldn't. Atheists think they know the truth. Even Reverend Pat and Rabbi Marsha aren't as dogmatic as that.

Baxter's black lab Betsy wanders into the room. Starting next week, Baxter is taking a leave of absence so he can be home. Betsy will be rapturous. The cats and the bird are mine; the dog belongs to Baxter. When I was a little girl, I was convinced that all cats were female, all dogs male. It was one of the stories that Ramona would later retell to torment me.

I should write to Ramona. No confession, no conversion. A letter of love. Love, no matter what. Mostly.

I sigh and open the two books again. Back to the L's. Back to those whose names won't vanish. I give Betsy a pat. There is pleasure in starting on an empty page.

Missing Person, Sister Night

NITA DISAPPEARED THE FIRST TIME ALMOST TWO years ago, the day before Valentine's Day. She packed her violin and a few clothes and left our folks' house in Santa Monica. She didn't leave a note, but Mom knew something was funny when she came home from her ladies' luncheon to find Nita's bedroom straight, even the bed made. She and Dad went to the police, but Nita was almost 19 and she clearly hadn't been kidnapped and she hadn't broken any laws, at least that anyone knew about.

I remember exactly what I was doing when they called me in San Francisco. I was grading ninth-grade science projects, Kenny Garcia's, to be exact, about flying fox bats, and I swallowed and put the cap on my green marking pen.

"Do you think she's come to the Bay Area?" I asked. Mom was blubbering so hard I couldn't understand her, and Dad got on the phone and said, "Lauren, we don't know what to think. Why would she hurt us like this?"

Imagining consequences was not one of Nita's talents, so I just said, "She probably didn't mean to, Dad. You know Nita."

But we really didn't know Nita. Each night, I remembered my childhood prayers, the ones Mom made us recite the years Nita and I shared a bedroom, and I uttered them and altered them to incorporate any god that might be listening. I pictured Nita at five, at eight, then at eleven when I was fourteen and we talked Mom into letting us both have our ears pierced. Nita had two brown braids that sometimes hid the tiny, gold music notes in her ear lobes. She was already playing in the school orchestra.

We heard nothing from Nita for six weeks. When she phoned me, John was giving me a backrub at my kitchen table. "Lauren?" she asked.

I gulped and fought to keep my voice even. I didn't want to scare her. "Where are you?"

"Paradise." She laughed. "New Orleans."

"Are you okay? New Orleans! Why New Orleans? What are you doing there?"

She laughed again. "Playing violin."

"Playing violin! Nita, we've all been frantic." I leaned against the refrigerator and nodded with my eyes at John.

"You shouldn't have been. We've been making enough to live on. We play on street corners."

"Who's we?"

"Bambi from my last semester orchestra class. You don't know her."

"Do *her* folks know where you are?"

"*Her* folks aren't as neurotic as *our* folks."

She wouldn't or couldn't give me a phone number, but she'd said she'd call me again and that I should assure Mom and Dad that she hadn't run off with Webster, her old high school boy-friend, which they had already ascertained, and that she didn't have any diseases, venereal or viral or *anything*, and she told me she loved me and hung up.

She called me twice more, once when she sounded lonely and a second time in the middle of the summer when she was so tired of the heat and humidity and probably Bambi too that she gave me an address. I sent her a ticket to fly home, and I flew home myself to make sure she got there. Sure enough, she received the welcome of the Prodigal Daughter, necks wet with tears and all, mine too. In the fall, she enrolled at Santa Monica College again, and the next spring she got a part-time job at a dry cleaner's which paid pretty well, and she found an apartment in Los Angeles with a woman from her sign language class and the delivery guy at the cleaner's, an arrangement Mom didn't like.

"We're all just *friends*," she'd say, but Mom worried about her sharing a bathroom with a bearded, tattooed 27-year-old. "He makes Webster look like a choir boy," Mom said. "Nita's still so secretive," she told me once on the phone, but then I was secretive too. Mom had pretty much given up on either one of us toeing the church line. Still, I had two college degrees and a respectable job and a mild, safe boyfriend, whom she had met and who lived in his own apartment, so Mom regarded me at least as an adult.

The second time Nita disappeared, she disappeared for good.

This time we thought we knew where she was going. She had bought a 20-year-old Volkswagen Beetle, almost as old, we joked, as she was, and she was going to drive it north to spend Thanksgiving with me. I was having a hard year. John had gone off to medical school in Florida and had fallen in love with one of his classmates and out of love, he said as gently as possible, with me. In an attempt to infuse positive change into my life, I had moved to Oakland to be closer to my school and some of my old college friends, but my apartment and the neighborhood were beige and bland, and at the end of each school day, I felt aimless and empty.

Nita was supposed to leave L.A. Wednesday morning. About two a.m., I decided that she must have got a late start, and I left my front door unlocked and went to bed. Thanksgiving morning, my throat pulsing and dry, I called her apartment. No answer. I shuddered at the thought of Mom's hysterics, but I called her and Dad anyway. They were over at Uncle Fred's house. They didn't know anything, and Mom's voice rattled in my ears. And then, amid the sounds and smells of Thanksgiving—neighbors' blaring TV football games, turkeys barbecuing in Webers on balconies—I telephoned the police.

We didn't have to wait as long as we did the first time. Friday, the Monterey County Sheriff's office called. The Volkswagen was in the bottom of a ravine along a windy and wet section of the coastal highway. Nita was seatbelted into the Volkswagen. She was dead.

I closed my eyes and sat absolutely still and took tiny sips of breath, which I counted. Then I called Uncle Fred and Aunt Helen and asked them to tell Mom and Dad. I called John in Florida, the first time I'd done it since he'd told me about the other woman in his life, and he kept saying, "Lauren, Lauren, I'm so sorry," and I kept saying, "I know." I called my principal at home and told him that I didn't want to return to school till after Christmas. He mumbled something about exceeding bereavement and personal leave, but sighed okay. I packed up my car and drove to the Monterey coroner's office.

THE FUNERAL WAS THE NEXT WEEKEND, IN THE MORMON chapel in Santa Monica, not because Nita ever set foot in the place after she turned 13, but because Mom and Dad knew everyone there, and the funeral was for them. The church ladies had filled our refrigerator with food and covered the sideboard with flowers. They held Mom's hand and dried her cheeks and their own.

On Monday, I left Mom, moderately sedated, on the living room couch with Aunt Helen and drove over to Nita's apartment. The week before, the Monterey County sheriff had given me her duffel and purse and keys. At the funeral Dad had told Nita's roommates, Guy and Barbara, to keep her furniture and kitchen stuff, mostly things she'd foraged from the folks' basement, but someone needed to go through her room. Dad had filled my backseat with folded boxes he'd salvaged from his office storeroom. I carried about seven of them up the stairs and along the outer walkway to apartment 29. This was a building with even less character than the one I lived in. Three pink-gray floors of apartments flanked a small, rectangular pool.

Apartment 29's living room apparently doubled as Guy's bedroom, and clothes and bedding were clumped on a twin bed against one wall. Underneath a mound of Levi's and sweaters, I thought I could see Uncle Fred's old military chest, and I recognized the brocaded loveseat that used to be in our dining room. I remembered the bean-bag pillow, but not the chairs, which must have been purloined from some other parents' basement.

I peeked into Barbara's bedroom and wondered how such an apparently neat person could live with Nita and Guy. The kitchen was fairly tidy too. The bathroom was a little steamy still, the shower curtain still wet and sticking together in big folds. It looked cleaner than the one I'd left in Oakland.

I knew Nita's room had to be behind the door with the poster of the Julliard Quartet. I put the boxes on the unmade bed and looked around. I set her violin case in the hall. It was a very good violin. I wondered what we should do with it.

I started with the clothes. I put together three of the boxes and slid open the closet door. Nita was about four inches shorter and two inches skinnier and four shades louder than I. The only thing I could see that I'd want for myself was the straw sun hat hanging on a nail. I knelt and, blowing the dust kittens off a pair of sandals, filled one box with shoes. I shook out and folded bright, patterned pants, blouses, skirts, some from hangers, some from heaps on the floor. I dragged a dusty brown shopping bag of letters out of the closet corner into the middle of the room.

Methodically, mechanically, I emptied drawers of sweaters, T-shirts, underwear, belts, scarves. Thinking this was the most order ever imposed upon Nita's possessions, I labeled the boxes, then went back to the car for more. I began on the books stuffed into the brick-and-board shelves. The clothes would go to Goodwill, but Dad would probably keep the books in the basement, even the sign language textbook with the torn cover.

I started on the dresser top. A plastic heart box full of change. A saucer of barrettes. A poodle-shaped earring hanger with dangling earrings. I fingered two pair of iridescent glass ones, then slipped them into my shirt pocket. She would want me to have them, to think of her whenever I wore them.

I sat on the bed, hugged myself, and shook. I would think of her anyway, for however long I would live. I kept my mouth closed and sniffed up sobs.

It had to be an accident. No evidence of drugs or drink. *Mom* was the one who fought depression. Nita wouldn't have chosen to put us all through this. But why did I keep asking myself, Why? And Who? And Where have you gone this time?

On her nightstand was a box of tissues, and I blew my nose and went back to the dresser. I reached for the pictures. An old one of Nita and Webster holding their surfboards at the beach. A small one of a clean-shaven man who had signed it, "Love, Roy." I remembered him, hovering about darkly at the funeral. A seven-by-five of the family, the four of us, in red felt stocking caps, in a kind of awkward chorus line in front of Uncle Fred's Christmas tree, four months after Nita had come home from New Orleans. I slid the case off of one of Nita's pillows, and I wrapped it around the pictures and tucked them into a cardboard box.

In the nightstand drawer was a brown leather-jacketed Bible, identical to one I had in my nightstand drawer—unwelcome Christmas gifts of our childhood, definitely in the same league as pajamas and socks. I sat again on the bed. Inside the front cover, Nita had printed her name in tiny neat letters, maybe when she was eight or nine. There were two ribbon markers, a blue scrap of paper, and a stiff business card, all acting as bookmarks. I thumbed through and was surprised to see verses underlined in pencil or in orange pen, scrawls in margins, even some inked stars. She hadn't made those stars when she was eight or nine. The orange pen lay in the front of the drawer.

The business card was that of a Janice DiPippo, counselor at the clinic for Women's Health Rights. It marked a page in Psalms, and in orange, Nita had underlined these words: "O Lord my

God, I cried unto thee, and thou hast healed me. Sing unto the Lord. For his anger endureth but a moment; weeping may endure for a night, but joy cometh in the morning." After "morning" was an orange star.

I used a blue marking pen and *my* Bible margins were full of question marks instead of stars. But there, in Proverbs, next to "There shall no evil happen to the just," there was an orange question mark. And here, next to "Trust in the Lord with all thine heart; and lean not unto thine own understanding," Nita had asked, in tiny letters, "Never?"

I stood by Nita's window, checking out the view. It was pretty dreary, another pink wall. The apartment across the driveway had posters instead of curtains, and Nita had had to look at the wrong side of the posters.

I was getting hungry. I'd have to make another trip anyway— to fit everything into my car. I had an ancient Volkswagen too, but a squareback, roomier than Nita's Beetle. We had planned to drive it up to Mendocino for Thanksgiving. And maybe we would have talked all night, the way we did that once, the time I flew back to Santa Monica for Christmas after my first semester of college.

I slipped the women's clinic card into my back pocket. Should I call this Janice DiPippo? If she knew anything, would she tell me? Probably not. There were rules, weren't there, to protect privacy?

I looked at the shopping bag in the middle of the floor and could see, even at a glance, some letters from me. I'd take the sack home. I didn't expect to find any answers—I'd become accustomed to living without answers. Maybe I'd find more questions. And maybe, somewhere in those pages or in her Biblical marginalia or reflected in her glass earrings or in my own heart, I'd find Nita, my lost little sister, and the morning joy.

Benares

I'VE BEEN TO ROME FIVE TIMES WITH FIVE DIFFERENT women," Byron said, not bragging, just stating a fact. He sprawled next to Lauren on a stone bench at the end of the shoreline trail. At the start of their run, they had been discussing the important places she had never been.

Lauren was breathing too hard to talk. When she shook her head, her long, licorice-colored pony tail swung against her neck, and she heard the tiny jingle of her glass earrings. She leaned over and retied the laces of her running shoes. "I will *not*," she said finally, "be the sixth."

And so the second day of the Christmas break, she turned her students' grades in to the office, and she and Byron flew across the Pacific, to India, to spend their honeymoon in the holiest place in the *eastern* world.

He had only taken one woman, before her, to Benares.

She had dreamt exotic dreams on Byron's shoulder on the long flights from San Francisco to Hong Kong to New Delhi, and then on the short flight to Varanasi. Varanasi was, she read in her guidebook, Benares' new and very old name. From the auto rickshaw they shared with a man and his son, she watched, her eyes and mouth open wide, people crowded onto the streets, buildings crowded next to the streets. At the hotel curb, she slung her pack over her shoulder and squinted over the chest-high wall at what seemed to be a small apartment building fronted by poplar-like trees.

"It looks very Western," she said, trying not to sound disappointed.

"We're splurging—seven dollars a night. My last time here I spent 75 cents, one for each bedbug. But you deserve better than a rope bed and a ceiling fan that squeaks all night."

"I want to see the *real* India."

Byron hoisted his pack onto his back, then pulled her close. He pointed across the street. "That's the *real* police station."

"How prudent," she said.

"How orderly," she said in the same tone when she saw the room—twin beds with ugly mustard coverlets and a small bathroom with a clean tub. She scowled and sat on the bed closer to the wall. In defiance of the travel guides and catalogues, she took off her sturdy walking shoes and her culottes, and slipped on an accordion-pleated skirt and sandals. She squeezed Byron's arm with one hand, clutched the guidebook in the other. "Let's walk down to the Ghats and the Ganges."

"Well, maybe we should work our way up to that. Early morning is best—you can see the pilgrims bathing and the water looks cleaner." He chewed his lower lip. "Look, the Mother India temple is about a five-minute walk. That'll be a good transition. And we can go inside."

She pursed her lips. "We should do the most important things first. If I die tonight, I want to have seen the Ghats."

He made a face. "Okay. The Ghats it is."

She kept her thumb on the page with the detailed map. Each street was narrower than the last. At first there was space for street vendors to lay out pottery and beads on blankets. Then stalls were crushed into the fronts of buildings. "The whole city," Byron said, mimicking the precise Indian accent by giving equal value to every syllable, "is open for business."

She stopped in front of a display of fabrics and let people push around her. "It is pure silk, *memsahib*," said a man in the same precise accent, "the best quality silk."

"How do I know it's real?" She tentatively touched a red swath.

"Oh it is pure silk, *memsahib*," said the man. "And a very good bargain too."

Byron pulled her after him, sliding her guide book into his pocket. "I know the way," he said, threading through arms waving, importuning; faces many shades of brown; people, so many people, in saris, turbans, baseball caps, t-shirts. He led her through the constricted, dark streets, barely as wide as sidewalks back home.

Suddenly there was blazing white light, and the Dasas-wamedh Ghat, the broad steps just visible through the layers of neon colors—people, canopies, flowers, silks—unfolded down to the river. She gasped and shivered though the air was hot. She had wanted to come because Byron, who had wandered around India for eight months after his bar exams, discarding all along the way little parts of his former Christian self, spoke of the country with a bewildering reverence. She had wanted to know what he knew. And she had wanted to come because Nita, her little sister, had told her, just a month before her car had careened down into the canyon of death, that she had wanted to make a pilgrimage to Benares.

It was dizzying, the late morning light ricocheting off the water, the slow and constant motion of flesh and fabric. It was hard to discern individuals. No one seemed to be alone. Most were stepping into and climbing back out of the river. Lauren had read about those who bathed and brushed their teeth and washed their clothing in the Ganges, even though there were almost certainly human and animal bodies and waste in the holy water. She saw no bodies floating, but they could be there, beneath the shimmering surface.

"It's something, huh?" he asked, and she realized he still had hold of her hand. She squeezed, hard.

"It's something," she repeated. "This is the *real* India, isn't it? I'm not just a proxy pilgrim for Nita. I'm a *real* pilgrim."

"It's real. We can walk up to the Manikarnika Ghat today. Tomorrow we can do the whole stretch from Manikarnika to Assi Ghat. We can do it by boat, if you'd like. Less real, but more pleasant."

She tried to drink it all in. A child approached, his hand extended in front of him. Byron put a few coins in the boy's palm, then shook his head when the boy gestured for more. Nearby, sitting cross-legged on the ground, was a bony, almost naked man, with a blood-red swatch on his forehead and an enormous, dirty turban covering his hair. He was absolutely still.

"Who is he?" she whispered. "What is he?"

"A sadhu. A wise man. He sacrifices all to seek enlightenment."

Since his eyes were closed, it seemed okay to stare. "How do you know when you've got enlightenment?"

"You're asking the wrong person. Keep an eye out for some-one who glows."

"*I* glow," she said and knew her excitement made it true. She was pretty sure she wasn't enlightened though. She hadn't felt enlightened even when the world made more sense, even when she thought there might be someone up there orchestrating it all.

Two women, filmy lavender saris wrapped around white T-shirts, slipped into the river.

"Is the water hot?" When Byron looked wary, she laughed. "I just want to touch it. I'll just touch it with my little finger." She pulled him close to the water. "I know. I'll touch it with my elbow. That way I won't contaminate anything." She knelt down and awkwardly dipped her elbow into the river. "It's very warm," she said after he pulled her up.

Three men, wearing nothing but loin cloths and necklaces, were lathering up on the lower steps. Their bodies glistened; they squinted to keep the soap out of their eyes; they chatted amiably and seemed unaware of a Western tourist gawking at them.

"I think you're the only person in India with freckles," Lauren told Byron as they climbed the stairs. A bas relief caught her eye. "That looks rather obscene."

"It's supposed to look phallic. This *is* the city of Shiva, and he seemed to favor artistic representations of his private parts. He's the god of reproduction, remember."

"And of destruction. A paradox." That was in the guidebook's chapter on religion. "Do they really believe in these gods?"

"How many Westerners do you know who really believe in *their* god? Well, besides your parents."

"It's easier to believe in gods that look like us. Two arms. One head."

"Why?" His eyes got a teasing look.

"I didn't say 'easy.' I said 'eas*ier*.' The familiar. You know."

"So some Hindus believe in Shiva and friends, and some Hindus are probably dubious. But I'll bet most people in the world believe in gods that don't look like people. In fact, they probably think that a god with only two arms is pretty puny."

Beside her appeared a bent-backed woman, her hair hidden in a stringy blue scarf. The woman said something unclear, and Byron reached across and offered coins, which the woman secreted in her sari. "Let's walk a little faster," Byron said. A man in a white dress shirt and a kind of sarong overtook them, didn't even glance their way. Two years ago, at her sister's funeral, she had felt surrounded by men in white shirts. Here, she was surrounded by patches of white in splashes of color. And the variety—even when she looked down. Some people wore shoes, some people wore sandals, some people walked on bare, blackened feet.

Lauren could see another Ghat, knee-high piles of logs and lumber on the steps. Smoke hung in the air. "This is Manikarnika," Byron said. "The wood is for a cremation. Looks like there was one earlier."

She nodded. "I remember. Only the rich can afford the wood. And then the ashes go into the river. The poor might just get singed a little. Then they go into the river too." She reached up and stroked his cheek. It was damp with sweat. "You want to be cremated. Do you want your ashes scattered in the Pacific?"

"I'm not fussy where. I just don't want a big coffin taking up space in the earth."

"I do. Well—I don't need a *big* coffin." She smiled at a man holding out marigolds. "Maybe six by three. With a headstone and my name and dates and maybe an azalea planted on top." They'd had musical notes engraved on Nita's stone. Lauren sighed. Nita would have been besotted with India. "I deserve some space in the earth," Lauren said. "After all, I glow." She poked Byron in the chest. "Don't grimace. These cremations aren't ecologically correct. I read about their smoke pollution and the devastation of their forests. And the river may be holy, but it certainly isn't wholesome."

"When I die, I'll try to evaporate," he said. "Or at least get incinerated with a catalytic converter."

Half a dozen men, some who seemed very old, some who seemed no older than her father, were hunched on a midlevel step, staring across and into the river. "What are *they* doing?" Lauren asked. "Meditating?"

"Waiting," said Byron.

"Waiting for what?"

"Waiting to die."

She looked, first at the men, then at Byron. "Are they sick? Are they in pain?"

Byron shrugged. "This is what they live for," he said, "to die at the Ganges in Benares."

When Lauren let out her breath, she realized she'd been holding it.

He took her hand again. "There's a hotel around here someplace with a sign that says, 'Stay—and die—in Varanasi.' That's shocking to an American, isn't it? The Brits say the difference between Americans and everyone else is that Americans think death is optional."

She tried to harrumph a small laugh, but it clotted in her throat. "They're more spiritual than we are, aren't they? The physical self must not matter much. So it's okay if the body is burned and if it's buried in sewage?"

He shrugged and smiled. "Physical rituals are still important. Where you die. Where that physical shell ends up. It's sanctified sewage."

Lauren looked more closely at the men on the step. Their eyes didn't seem focused. They seemed to be wilting. Maybe they would melt to death here. A pack of children approached, their greedy little hands reaching out to her. The flower seller came closer, offering her a necklace of yellow-orange marigolds. It's for my pyre, she thought suddenly, and I *haven't* come here to die. She backed away. The heat made the air quiver and she half expected a genie or a sadhu or a god—one of theirs or maybe her parents'—to rise up and whisper instructions.

And then it was all too much—too many colors, too much heat, too many people, too little space. The light seemed to swirl smoke and she gulped hot air and her chest felt tight. She dropped Byron's hand. The buildings, the people leaned in towards her. She turned away and began to run. She squeezed through the crowd, into a narrow street and pushed against men and women who seemed to be begging or selling. She scraped against the corner of a building, tried to get to a bigger space, to get air to breathe. Her sandals slapped against the stones. The street seemed to be getting more cramped; there were more encumbrances—a gaunt cow, brass objects laid out on a swatch of material, signs with strange letters. Byron was calling somewhere behind her, but she couldn't stop. Where was she running? Maybe she could find a park somewhere, with trees and grass and air and space and solitude, and she could collapse onto the lawn and rest there till her heart stopped pounding and she could breathe again.

A bicycle rickshaw blocked the way and she stopped, pawing the ground with one foot, looking about frantically. A curtain was bunched to the side of a doorway. Inside it looked cool and dark. She took a breath and stepped in.

Two men were squatting on the floor on either side of a low table and a chessboard. The older man was pondering his move and seemed not to notice her, but the younger man looked up and smiled. She leaned against the wall and watched. Her breaths became more even. The older man moved a castle. The younger man leaned back and closed his eyes. When he sat up, he moved his queen. "Checkmate," he said.

The older man cocked his head to the side. He exhaled and turned to Lauren. "*Memsahib*, you are American?" he asked. "Do you play?"

"What? Chess?" She slid down the wall onto the floor next to the table. It felt good to be out of the light, to be on the cool floor. "I play," she said. "Do I get the winner or the loser?"

"The winner," said the younger man, shifting around opposite her and replacing the pieces on the board. "You first."

The board looked deliciously open. She moved a side pawn. It had been years since she had played chess, and then it was with Uncle Baxter, during the months Aunt Charlotte was busy dying. But for now it felt reassuring to sit in the quiet and move the white pieces on a familiar board. The two kings looked a little like sadhus in turbans.

The older man stepped out into the street, and Byron stepped in.

She looked up. "My husband," she said. My husband, she thought. It was the first time she had said that phrase. She liked saying it.

The young man moved a knight. "Sit down, *sahib*," he said with a smile, and Byron sat down beside Lauren. "Are you okay?" Byron whispered.

"I'd better be." She moved another pawn. "All these guys—and this gal," she motioned towards the queen, who looked like a taller sadhu, "are counting on me to lead them into battle."

"Ah," said the young man. He reached his hand over a pawn, then retracted it and leaned back. He rested his chin on the backs of his knuckles and contemplated the board.

Lauren grinned at Byron, whose eyes were full of wonder. "Maybe I'll even win," she murmured. "I've got a god with two powerful arms on my side."

Carma

Out of the Woods

HERE THEY GO, CARMA WITHOUT HER CANE—SHE'LL hang onto Dan if her legs give way—through the glass doors into the maze of parents and teenagers and little brothers and sisters, milling, waving, shrieking, whimpering.

"I can't find the camera," screeches a frantic woman up to her elbows in a canvas bag. Stepping serenely around the woman, Carma and Dan raise eyebrows at one another and attach themselves to the end of the line that snakes through the lobby to the locked high school auditorium. *Their* camera is around Dan's neck. From Carma's canvas bag erupts an enormous bouquet of yellow roses.

"Oooh, roses," a voice behind them squeals. "Who're they for?"

Carma turns and smiles. "Our daughter."

A girl in tight Levi's and a sequined halter smiles back. "What's her name? What's she playing?" A rhinestone, or maybe another sequin, pierces her tongue. She is tugging on the belt loop of a torpid boy with chartreuse hair.

"Sophie Cusins," Carma says. "She plays the witch."

"Sophie!" The boy stirs and becomes alert. "Sophie's in honors English. She's way cool."

"And the witch!" the girl adds.

"She's been rehearsing for it all her life," says Dan.

"Says her father." Carma wrinkles her nose at him. The girl lets escape a thin, sequiny laugh.

The doors are pushed open, late, as usual, and the throng streams in, the teenagers coalescing in bunches and yelling at each other. Carma and Dan take their usual places, on the aisle, right side, third row, where Dan's fullback frame won't block too many views. From here, he can bound down to the front at the end of each act, kneel, and snap away.

Carma settles into the rickety folding seat. Even though she left work early and tried to nap this afternoon, her joints throb. She takes a breath and composes her face carefully. "Look at the bright side," those insipid self-help manuals say. The bright side of rheumatoid arthritis is that Sophie has never had to deal with a zealous stage mother like Alicia Sanchez, standing over there in the middle section, flailing her lumpy arms around. Her daughter Becky looks a lot like her—meaty, freckled. Becky usually gets those character parts. She's Jack's mother in this production. She wanted to be the witch. But in *this* version of the fairy tales, Sondheim's, the witch turns into a gorgeous vamp, and Sophie has all the equipment to be a gorgeous vamp. She sings better than Becky too. Carma doesn't understand why that is. Sophie doesn't seem to work very hard at it. Unlike her big sister. When Grace was in these musicals, she was always crouched over the piano, practicing her part, and her part was never a big part. But Sophie—every evening she sits at that same piano bench, sings her songs through once, then curls up on her bed with her phone.

"Hello Dan, Carma." It's Natalie Green, motioning towards the seats to her right. "Those taken? May we sit there?"

Dan stands and Carma swivels her legs to the side, wincing at the pain in her hip. Natalie and her husband—Ted? Tom?— shake Dan's hand, try to suck in their bodies, and squeeze by. Natalie plops down next to Carma so the husband has to press past everyone to get to the seat next to the wall.

"We almost didn't make it." Natalie fans herself with her program. "We had to arrange for the Sorensons to pick Billy up from soccer, and the babysitter wasn't ready when Tim went to get her, and then Peggy had a tantrum. Oh you brought Sophie flowers!" Carma's bag is wedged under the seat in front, the flowers spilling out, one crushed by Natalie and Tim-Tom-Ted. "We should have brought Craig something. What do you bring for boys?"

Carma tries to remember what part Craig plays. One of the princes certainly; he's such a pretty boy, Sophie has told them with a dismissive lilt in her voice. "Balloons maybe," Carma says, "but I don't know where you'd keep them during the show."

"Oh balloons." Natalie makes a face. "I didn't think of balloons. Craig says Sophie is just marvelous. She's so talented. You know there's a great group of kids at church now, just like when Grace was in high school. Sophie would really fit in."

Sophie would not fit in, Carma thinks, but she says mildly, "Sophie's free to go to church if she wants to. Any church."

Natalie pretends not to hear the addition. "Craig could give her a ride. We let him take a car. He's so responsible."

"She can always get a ride with Dan." Carma peers through her glasses at her program and checks Sophie's name. For a change, it's spelled correctly.

"We'd love it if you came too," Natalie says hopefully. "If you feel well enough. And you know we make tapes for people who can't come to meetings."

Carma forces a smile. "Dan relays the most interesting bits." She feels Dan's light touch on her shoulder. Knowing how heavy his arm can be, he rests it mostly on the back of her chair. She turns away from Natalie, and the auditorium is suddenly black except for the music light on the piano.

The music teacher drops her hands onto the keyboard and starts to play. When the curtains are drawn, Cinderella and Jack and the Baker are all lamenting their losses. The music is shrill yet sweet, thinks Carma, like sweet and sour. She's been listening to Sophie's songs for weeks. They all sound alike.

The preliminaries over, Red Riding Hood has skipped off into the woods, and Sophie steps forward to witchily harass the Baker with the salient points of his family history and the reason it is to end with him: she caught his father rooting through her rutabagas. "Don't ever never ever mess around with my greens," she spits out, and the audience snickers and guffaws.

She's always been good at working the audience. Now she is offering to reverse the curse—for a price. She controls this scene, Sophie does. Ah, but Carma knows that before the act is over, the witch will be only a beautiful woman stripped of her magical powers, at which point she'll turn her full attention to the creaky seats and work her *theatrical* sorcery on those in them.

Carma never worries about Sophie forgetting her lines or even losing her composure if she misses a note. When you belt them out, what's a wrong note here and there? This isn't opera. She and Dan just lean back and enjoy the show, wincing only at the other kids' performances. When Natalie's son squeaks out his adoration of Rapunzel, Natalie and Tim exchange little moans and shuffle their feet.

That's how it was with Grace. "You know," Dan said once, "it was more of an achievement for Grace to sing in an octet than for Sophie to be the star."

Carma understands Grace's inclination to gravitate to the back of the stage; she understands Grace's penchant to please. But she can't understand how Grace could put college on hold to marry someone as sweetly bland as Ryan. And a baby now before she is 21. The baby though, Carma smiles to think about Bradley, fat-cheeked and sunny, she calls him Buddha-ley, the baby is spectacular.

"How is Grace?" Natalie asks after the Act I curtain drops and the whistles and foot stomping die down. Carma does happen to have two shiny snapshots of Grace and the baby lying on the red and blue sailboat quilt that Carma and Sophie, mostly Sophie, had put together and tied.

"He's gorgeous." Natalie stands and shows the pictures to Tim.

"He is, isn't he?" Carma pushes herself to her feet.

"They're still in Utah?"

Carma nods.

"When does her husband graduate?"

"He's got two more years." Alicia Sanchez is pushing her way towards them. Dan has stepped across the aisle and is shaking someone's hand.

"Sophie's great," Alicia gushes. "She's got the part down pat. Bernadette Peters couldn't do it better."

"Becky's doing well too," Carma says. "They're all doing well." She stands back so Natalie isn't excluded.

"And Craig. Craig's doing just fine," Alicia says, without conviction. "Oh, there!" She points at someone and swooshes up the aisle.

Natalie hands the photos back to Carma. "They're very different, your daughters."

"Yes."

"Is Sophie," she hesitates, "more like you?"

Carma laughs. "I don't think either one is very much like me."

"Sophie has your lovely thick hair."

"With pink streaks instead of gray."

"Kids shout with their hair now, neon colors, everything." Natalie sighs. "I don't know how I'd raise mine without the church." Carma realizes Natalie has briefly forgotten her. Then she remembers and laughs nervously. "Their world is so different from the world I grew up in."

Carma lowers herself into her seat. "Where did you grow up?"

"Idaho. Rexburg." Glancing at the children rushing back to front-row center, Natalie sits down. "You know, my kids aren't like me either. To get up on a stage in front of the whole school and sing with nothing but a piano behind you—I would have died first. I was never any good at anything that people might watch. Sports. One summer I played tennis every morning and by the end of August I was still missing half the balls and hitting the other half past the base line."

Carma has to nod. "Sounds like me. I tried volleyball once. And badminton." She laughs. "I was always a klutz. And that was even before the arthritis."

Natalie lowers her voice. "How long have you have had it?"

"Twenty years." Carma looks at her hands, covers one with the other. "I was diagnosed right after I had Grace. I couldn't get out of bed."

"Is it—inherited?"

Carma shrugs. "It seems to run in families. The girls *probably* won't get it, but you never know." She pauses. "I'll never forgive myself if they get it."

Natalie looks alarmed. "There's nothing you could do."

"I could have *not* had them."

"No," Natalie says. "You had to have them. We can't any of us know what will happen to our kids. We just pray for the best." Her voice goes up as if this is a question.

Carma answers it with a sigh.

"Is it—do you hurt all the time?"

"No." Carma stops herself from making an accordion fan out of her program. She wants to make copies for the grandparents. "Sometimes it's in remission. I felt great when I was pregnant with Sophie. But afterwards it was a lot worse."

Natalie touches her very lightly on the arm. "I didn't know it was so bad. Do you hurt right now?"

Carma doesn't want to itemize, quantify her pain. Suddenly she doesn't want to talk at all. "You get used to it."

Dan creaks in the seat beside her. The theater darkens. Behind them, she can hear two boys talking. "I know Sophie," one says. "Oh yeah? What do you know?" asks the other. Carma holds her breath. "She's all right." Carma lets her breath out as the piano starts the monotonous jingle that begins Act II.

Sophie as Witch is mother-by-bribery, and she is quite a convincing mother, especially after the Giantess squashes her Rapunzel. Carma's glasses steam up as Sophie sings out, "Children don't listen." She is surprised at her tears and can see that Dan's cheeks are wet too.

Their daughters have listened, but it was hard to know what they heard. She and Dan didn't shout. Dan, in fact, always sounded calm, whereas she always sounded, at least to her own ears, whiny. Dan didn't pretend to have answers for all her questions. He honestly didn't have questions himself. "I don't know about religion, organized or disorganized," she wept after he baptized Sophie. "I just don't believe it anymore. I've tried to believe it. I'm not saying it's not true. It's true for you. I even want it to be true for you. You should do what you have to do. And I should do what I have to do. I have to stop pretending it works for me."

Eight years ago now. That whole year the arthritis flared and nothing helped and nobody slept well. Grace was sad. Carma's mother was sad. Dan's parents, visiting from Seattle, were sad. But Dan was shocked when Carma asked if he wanted to divorce her and find someone who could believe as he believed, who could join him in that hierarchical hereafter. And she was grateful that he protected her, as he must have done, from visits by those who wanted to persuade her that she was ruining her family's chances for salvation. "Take the girls to church," she had said. But given the choice, Sophie usually opted to "stay home with Mom."

In Carma's childhood home, it was her father who didn't go to church. The common pattern—believing, determined women; rebellious or indifferent men. But at least she had some kind of precedent. Carma did what her father had done—if Grace were giving a talk or getting an award or singing in a group, then Carma would go.

But she couldn't go everywhere Grace went. When Grace got that scholarship, the one she gave up after a single year, and set off for Provo, Carma surmised, correctly, that her daughter would eventually be married in a ceremony she could not witness. Twenty-three years after she and Dan had driven quietly to Arizona to get married so that no one would feel left out, Grace and Ryan had driven quietly to Utah to marry so that Carma wouldn't feel left out. "You go," she had insisted to Dan, and he went. A week later, at the reception in Carma and Dan's garden, Grace, in the simple white dress she and Sophie had sewn together, greeted guests with a tranquility that astonished her mother, that separated them in a way the sadness couldn't. Ryan's true-believing family treated—still treat—Carma with profuse, bewildering courtesy.

The light is focused on Sophie, singing, "It doesn't matter now, it's the last midnight." She is singing as if it matters very much. "I'm not good, I'm not nice, I'm just right, I'm the witch," she croons. "I'm what no one believes."

Sophie is not sexually active, Carma is almost sure, not yet. She hasn't had Grace's reasons for chastity, but she has held onto it, up to now. How will she feel when Sophie lets it go? Dan will be devastated. Dan is good. Grace is good. Sophie is good. And she, even *she* is good. Probably. Where do our ideas of good-ness come from, Carma wonders. Can anyone get there all on her own, no current church or past church, no great mentors or influential parents, no Dostoevskys or Kierkegaards? Can she get there? And where oh where is there?

Dan takes her hand and holds it, touches lightly the fused joint in her ring finger. The finger is swollen so that if she did want to take off her wedding band, someone would have to cut the gold.

"Careful the things you say," Sophie is singing with the Baker. "Children will listen." The rest of the cast is singing now, chil-dren themselves, children playing children and children playing adults. Natalie and Tim's prince son Craig swells up his chest and looks, indeed, very handsome. Sophie and Cinderella and the Baker are in the center, and their eyes are shiny and their voices sweet and strong. The piano is barely audible as they all sing, then shout, "Happily ever after!"

No one believes it of course, the happily-ever-after, but the audience has been transported out of the woods. They stand and shriek and clap and stomp and whistle. Dan is on his knees at the front of the aisle, with four or five other parents, snapping pictures, offering homage. The curtain closes, then opens again, and the whistles and applause resume.

Natalie sits back down beside Carma. "You must be proud."

Carma nods and smiles. "You too."

"Yes."

"Go on ahead. We wait till the aisles are clear." The cast will be in the lobby, surrounded by ecstatic friends. Natalie and Tim edge by her. Up front, Dan is staggering under a bear hug from the Baker's mother, a willowy woman, pretty, young enough to have given birth to the Baker when she was 14. A hug like that would break Carma in two. I don't have to worry about Dan, Carma thinks. Why is it she doesn't worry? Is it because of the church that separates them? Is it the code that one is responsible for a partner, no matter how she changes? Neither of them had envisioned that she would be unable to pick up either of their babies, that at times she would be fat-faced and dopey from the drugs, that she would be taken apart by surgeons, that some days she would stare out the window at the laurel hedge and disappear into it for hours. And neither of them had envisioned her arthritic soul.

Natalie returns and crouches beside Carma's seat. "I was just thinking—I guess you've had blessings," she hesitates, "to ease the pain?"

"A lot of blessings," says Carma. She pats Natalie's hand. "And maybe they helped."

As Natalie stands, she brushes Carma's cheek with her lips. "I'll be praying for you," she says, and, eyes lowered, she runs back to the lobby.

Carma says suddenly, silently, to Natalie, to Dan, to God, if there is a God, even to herself, "Yes. Pray for me." Then she smiles at Dan, now disentangled from the Baker's mother. She hands him the bag of yellow roses and pushes up out of her chair. "Shall we make merry?"

"Let's," he says and offers her his arm, and they set out, stumbling just a little, up the empty aisle.

Acute Distress, Intensive Care

BARB'S DYING, CARMA THINKS, AND SHE STEADIES herself against the chest of drawers as Dan, kneeling beside his sister's bed, strokes Barb's face. Barb's head seems to be rocking slightly on the pillow. Her eyes are closed, her mouth open.

"Sis?" Dan asks. "Barb, what's wrong?" He turns and speaks over his shoulder to Carma. "She's on fire. Come feel."

But instead, Carma leaves her cane in the hall and brings wet washcloths from the bathroom, ice cubes in a dishtowel from the kitchen downstairs. She steps unsteadily around Barb's awful dachshund Buddy, who whimpers and paces at the foot of the bed.

"I'll call 911," Carma says.

Barb's eyes open wide. For an instant she looks at them in terror, then shuts her eyes and smiles. "Danny," she sighs. "You've come."

Carma brings juice from the refrigerator, a straw from the cupboard. Dan holds Barb's head so she can take little sips. Carma reaches for the phone on the nightstand.

"Wait," Dan says. "Sis? Do you know what's wrong? Can we call your doctor?"

Barb dribbles a little yellow juice down her chin. "I don't want," she has to breathe between words, "you to call anyone." Her voice is barely audible. "Don't."

"How long have you been sick?" Dan asks. "Do you hurt anywhere?"

"Buddy," she pants. "Carma." She takes a breath. "Feed him?"

Next to the doggy door between the kitchen and the deck are two empty bowls, orange and blue. Carma puts water in one. While she looks through the cupboard for something to put into the other, she hears Buddy slurping. Barb is very, very sick, Carma thinks, or she would have fallen down the stairs to feed Buddy. She loves that dog more than she loves almost anyone, certainly more than the neighbors who, last year, circulated a petition about his barking and biting. Carma glances at the ashtray and the pack of cigarettes on the table. But Barb doesn't love him more than cigarettes. Buddy has asthma and wheezes all the time, and the vet has suggested that if Barb didn't smoke around him, maybe he wouldn't need all that medicine. There are two trays of prescription bottles next to the cigarettes, one for Buddy, one for Barb—hers probably for depression, anxiety, sleeplessness, maybe back pain—her usual complaints.

Dan is at the kitchen door. "I'll take care of the dog," he says. "She wants you to help her clean up."

"She needs a hospital," Carma whispers. "Call an ambulance."

Dan shakes his head. "That would just alarm her. She asked specifically that we not call an ambulance."

Carma sighs. "At least call Amy. Maybe she's talked to her mom. She probably knows her doctor at least. Here." She takes her phone from her purse. "Amy. Here."

"Amy lives more than an hour away."

"Call her. Please. And call Grace and tell her we aren't sure now when we'll see them."

Barb is breathing heavily, inhaling with a kind of gulp. It smells bad in here, Carma thinks, and she finds a small plastic tub under the bathroom sink and fills it with warm water. She sets it on a chair next to her sister-in-law's bed and brings in an armload of washcloths and towels.

"Carma," Barb says slowly, "Clean gown."

I know how to do this, Carma says to herself. When she could hardly move, the months after Grace's birth and then Sophie's and the surgeries and all those other times, the home nurse would do then what she will do now. She pushes up the sleeves of her pullover and takes a deep breath. She rolls Barb gently towards the center of the bed, pulls off the soiled gown, washes Barb's body and the bottom sheet too, best she can, towels her dry, works a big dry towel under her, and maneuvers arms and head into a fresh kimono she finds in the closet. On Barb's right rump is an astonishing tattoo of a vermillion-throated hummingbird. Who would have guessed?

"Carma," Barb says when she has finished. Her eyes are intent now. Her eyes seem to say, "You know what's going to happen, don't you?"

And Carma does know.

CARMA AND DAN HAD NO WARNING. THEY DROVE THE rental car straight to Barb's house from the Salt Lake airport, planning to take Dan's sister to lunch before setting off to Provo to see Grace and Ryan and darling Bradley and the new grand-baby. Buddy greeted them with agitated howls when they rang the bell and finally pushed open the unlocked front door. There was no answer to their calls, and Dan had bolted up the stairs to the bedroom.

Two, no, three days ago they'd phoned her from California, set up the lunch date. Barb sounded fine then. Well, as fine as she had sounded in the past five years. Ever since the divorce, she'd been so deflated, as if all her energy were whistling out through a little leak somewhere. But she'd planned to drive down to Provo with Amy for the baby blessing on Sunday.

Barb needs more than a winter job, Dan often says, though he doesn't consider renting out skis at Alta a real job. Summers, she's on call for vacation replacement and sales weekends at a Salt Lake sporting goods store. That jerk she was married to did agree to a handsome enough settlement so she can work when she wants to, and the house, with its crumbling basement floors and unreliable air conditioner, is in her name.

"Left a message for Amy," Dan says when Carma returns to the kitchen. "And Grace says to let her know what's happening."

"Dan," she says. "Your sister is *really* sick. We have to get her to a hospital. You and I can't carry her out to the car. She can't sit in a waiting room. We *have* to call an ambulance."

"I don't want to," Dan says. "Not when she doesn't want it."

"We'll have to stay with her every minute," Carma urges. "She needs critical care, and we don't know how to do that."

Dan squeezes his temples with his left hand. "Okay," he says at last. "But tell them no sirens."

Carma tells them no sirens, and the ambulance comes quietly, but two fire trucks spot and join the action, and the blare might resurrect the dead. Out the window, Carma can see the cul-de-sac crammed with vehicles, and several big uniformed men are suddenly at the door. She scoops up Buddy, oddly subdued, and shuts him in the laundry room. He immediately starts to yelp.

Barb looks betrayed, but a little relieved, too. The paramedics have her propped up and are doing an oxygen thumb test and taking her temperature. "How old are you?" the one with a laptop asks.

"Forty-five," Barb says. Add three years, thinks Carma.

"Do you smoke?"

Barb has to catch her breath. "Used to," she says.

"How long ago did you stop?"

Barb shrugs. "A couple of weeks?" presses the paramedic.

Barb closes her eyes and nods.

IN THE CURTAINED-OFF CUBBY AT THE ER, THE ONLY thing to sit on is the doctor's wheeled stool, so Carma pushes it close to the bed and takes hold of Barb's limp hand. Dan is in the hall, talking to Amy on the phone. Barb's bed has been raised to a half-sitting position, and she looks pretty in the clean kimono. She is connected to a black box and a transparent bag and oxygen. Every few seconds something beeps, and numbers change on the black box. A fan pulses somewhere.

"I'm keeping you," Barb's voice quavers, "from seeing the new baby."

"Don't worry," Carma says. "We'll get there."

"I forgot," Barb pauses to breathe, "her name."

"Camilla. They call her Cammy."

Barb closes her eyes, exhales as if through mud. "Like Carma."

"Kind of."

Dan touches his sister's arm. "Amy is on her way," he says.

A doctor hustles in, stands at the foot of the bed. "You, my lady," he announces to Barb, "have full-blown pneumonia. We're finding you a room."

Barb makes a face. "What," she whispers, "about Buddy?"

"That magnet on the fridge," Dan says, "that's the kennel you used when you went on that cruise?"

"He liked it there," Barb murmurs.

"We'll take him after they have you settled."

"You," a weak cough, "don't have to stay."

"We'll stay until Amy comes." Dan squeezes Barb's shoulder.

Carma nods. Suddenly she feels very hungry. It has been a long time since breakfast. And a hymn is pounding in her head— one they used to sing in church. "Master, the Tempest Is Raging." She doesn't know if they still sing it. "Whether the wrath of the storm-tossed sea," BUM bum bum, BUM bum bum, "demons or men or whatever it be . . ." a sort of bass chant echoed by the beeping machines and the wheeled whooshes in the hallway and Dan's soft words to his sister.

CAMILLA IS SILKY AND PINK AND SMELLS LIKE TALC. GRACE places her into Carma's arms, and Carma kisses the reddish fuzz on her granddaughter's scalp. Bradley is opening the presents they brought him, board books and a quilted bird house filled with small stuffed birds. Pushed forward by his mother, he takes hold of Carma's knee. "Thank you, Gamma," he says. "Can I play with this?" He has appropriated Carma's flowered purple cane, which is taller than he is. He clearly prefers it to the bird house.

His other grandmother, who lives just a few miles away, is Nana, the number one grandma. It is she who has been spoiling Bradley and helping with laundry and filling up the fridge with food. Knowing of the arrival of the less robust grandmother today, the church ladies have brought over dinner, and Ryan has stuck it into the oven to reheat. Lasagna, by the smell of it. Carma and Dan are ravenous, having eaten nothing but a couple of breakfast bars Carma had stowed in her purse.

"So Aunt Barb has pneumonia." Grace moves Ryan's books and laptop to the couch and sets forks and knives on the table. She is wearing black capris and, Carma notices, has already lost most of her baby fat.

"I'm sure it's worse," says Ryan, "for someone who has smoked so long." He talks out of one side of his mouth; in the other he chomps on a baby carrot like a cigar.

"If she'd lived in the Bay Area," Dan says, "she wouldn't still smoke. You should see the smokers on their break when it rains. They have to be so many feet from the doorways of buildings. They skulk around trying to find a place to keep dry."

Carma wiggles Cammy's tiny toes. "I can picture Barb smoking and skulking," she says.

"I think Barb only smokes to show Utahns that she isn't a Mormon anymore." Dan is on the floor now, teasing Bradley, who is still wound around Carma's cane. "Amy has been after her for years to stop."

Carma catches Grace's sidelong glance at Ryan. Carma, too, isn't a Mormon anymore. But she's about as likely to start smoking as she is to take up glacier-scrambling.

"Sophie calls you often?" Carma makes it a question and an answer. She suddenly thinks—and my younger daughter isn't a Mormon anymore either. And maybe that's *my* doing.

"She calls Wednesday afternoons," Grace says. "She doesn't have classes then. I think she's a little lonely. But she's pretty absorbed in school. She has a small part in a play, I forget its name. And Manhattan, well she says there's always more to do than there's time."

"It's the *The Cherry Orchard*," Dan says. "She usually calls us Saturday mornings while she's doing her laundry. Or we call her. Let's call her now." He extracts the cane from Bradley's grasp and tousles his hair. "We can give her a first-hand account of her new niece." He winks at Bradley. "And, of course, her old nephew."

THEY ARE STAYING AT A MOTEL. CARMA INSISTED. EVERY-one will sleep better. Otherwise Grace and Ryan would be on an air mattress in the living room, next to the baby's crib, and she and Dan would be in their bed, and everyone would be using one bathroom, and to take a shower, you'd have to take all the rubber toys out of the tub. Besides, she gets up a couple of times in the night, and on their last trip she stumbled and cried out and woke everyone, even Bradley in his tiny bedroom.

But Carma and Dan don't sleep well at the motel either. About 5 a.m., Amy telephones. "Mom's taken a turn for the worse," she says. "She's in ICU. Her fever spiked to 105. They have this BiPAP mask on her to give her more oxygen." Amy has spent the whole night there, catching naps on a couch in a small waiting room.

"We'll make it there in an hour and a half," says Dan, and they almost do.

Barb can't talk because of the plastic mask. She seems to be dozing, but she looks up when Dan presses her arm, the arm that isn't connected to the IVs. She seems somewhat lost, scared.

Instead of the pretty kimono, she is wearing an ugly white-with-blue-diamonds hospital gown.

"Why don't you go back to your mom's?" Carma says to Amy. "Get some sleep. We'll be here." Amy nods. "And eat something," Carma adds.

"Would you like me to give you a blessing?" Dan asks Barb. She seems to bob her head. "There's probably someone who can help me," he whispers to Carma. "I saw a chaplain's office on the first floor, next to all that St. Whosits stuff. Even in an Episcopalian Hospital, there must be Mormons around. This is Utah, after all."

Carma takes his chair when he leaves it. She holds Barb's hand. "The baby looks like Sophie, I think," she says. "Sophie with reddish hair." Will Cammy be docile and tranquil like Grace? Or uninhibited, impatient like Sophie? Sophie's a doting aunt though, makes a big fuss over Bradley when they're all together. Carma smiles at Barb, whose gaze drifts around the room. Then Barb lifts her other hand, the one attached to the arm encumbered by tubes, raises her hand to her face. Her fingers are separated, and she slowly moves her hand side to side. She is smoking, Carma realizes, an imaginary cigarette.

Dan returns with a short, bearded man in Levi's and a sweatshirt. "My wife Carma," he says, "and," motioning to the bed, "my sister Barbara. This is Ray. He's the chaplain. Mormon chaplain." Dan takes a small vial of oil from Ray and puts a drop on Barb's head. Barb looks a little alarmed, so Carma squeezes her hand harder and tries to look reassuring. The two men cover the oil with their crossed hands and close their eyes. Carma realizes Barb might be wondering what they are doing to her hair, to her head. The last time men put their hands on Barb's head like that, she was probably eight years old, after she'd been baptized. Sometimes, like when she has surgery, Carma lets Dan put oil and his hands on her own head. It makes him feel better.

"If it be thy will," Dan is saying, "restore sweet Barbara to health."

If there is a God, Carma thinks, whom does he *will* to health, to life? How does he decide?

"And give her peace," Dan is saying. Barb seems to have slid into sleep. Peace, repeats Carma. A-men.

IT'S DARK WHEN THEY GET BACK TO GRACE'S APARTMENT. Ryan and Bradley have had their dinner—Ryan is off at the library to study for an exam, but Grace puts on the table a different lasagna and eats with her parents. Bradley is allowed to stay up an extra hour so Dan can give him rides on his camel back and so Carma can read to him and calm him down. Carma holds the baby, changes her diaper, hums to her. "'Give,' says the little stream," she remembers, "as it hurries down the hill."

There is another phone call in the early morning at the motel. Amy has spent a second night at the hospital. The BiPAP wasn't giving Barb enough oxygen; in order to get tubes down her, the doctors put her into a coma. "So there's no need for you to rush up," Amy says. "She's stable and she isn't really conscious. Every hour they wake her just a little, to prove they can, I guess." Her voice trembles.

At her daughter's apartment, Carma makes oatmeal for breakfast. "We're not much help to you," she tells Grace, who is nursing the baby.

"You're a help to Aunt Barb—or anyway Amy. Think how hard it would be for Amy if she had to deal with this by herself."

"I don't know. I guess we have to be there. At least your dad has to be there. Maybe I should let him go alone."

"Mom," she says, "you are a help to Dad."

This time they don't hurry so much. They pack sandwiches and fruit. As Dan drives, no faster than the speed limit, Carma finds a classical music station on the radio. She practices her breathing exercises, then rubs Dan's neck and touches his cheek.

"She's my *little* sister," Dan says. "I should have tried to stay closer to her."

Carma thinks about, but doesn't mention, the hummingbird tattoo.

After sending Amy to Barb's house to sleep, they settle themselves in the hospital room. Barb seems restless, as if she were having bad dreams, as if she hurts. Maybe she does—the tubes must feel awful. That's why they put her into a coma, isn't it?

Dan sits, holds Barb's hand, then stands, then paces. A young Indian doctor appears at the door.

"What's happening?" Dan asks. The doctor motions them outside. "I am Dr. Gill," he says, and shakes their hands. He looks at Carma's cane.

"R.A.," she answers the question his eyes ask. "Can she hear us?"

"Perhaps on some level," the doctor says in precisely enunciated English. "She is agitated."

"Maybe it's nicotine withdrawal," Carma offers. "She smokes a pack or two a day."

"Ah," says the doctor. "We can give her a nicotine patch. Her lungs are like paper." He clears his throat. "It is more than pneumonia now. It is acute respiratory distress syndrome. We call it ARDS."

Dan catches his breath. "And the prognosis?"

Dr. Gill raises his thick eyebrows. "About two-thirds of patients with ARDS survive. We will know more in a day or two." He speaks very softly. "She may have some brain damage. Her blood and her brain have been starved for oxygen. You and her daughter need to talk about the different alternatives."

"If she pulls through, could she live on her own?" Carma asks. "Could she go back to her home?" She looks over at Dan, whose eyes seem unfocused. "Her house has stairs."

The doctor sighs. "If she recovers enough to leave here, I would guess she would have to stay several months at a rehabilitation center or an assisted living facility, maybe even a nursing home. I cannot imagine her living alone."

"No cigarettes," Carma says. "No Buddy. Her dog," she explains to the doctor, "her dreadful little dog."

Amy returns to the hospital in the middle of the afternoon. She has washed her hair and has put on one of Barb's bright blue sweaters. She's older than Sophie, younger than Grace, not as pretty as either one, Carma thinks, but she has luminous skin and a sensual awareness that her cousins lack. She has a will to do well that she didn't seem to inherit from her mom or dad. She was raised in a religion-free home, one of the few things her parents came to agree on. She's a court reporter in Ogden, types on those little machines, makes a much better salary than a social worker, even if Carma were still a full-time social worker.

While Amy and Dan go to the chaplain's office, Carma stays with Barb, whose mouth is stretched out of shape by the cruel tube. She seems calmer now that she is sporting a nicotine patch. If only they could have got her to wear one of those before— Carma takes a motel bottle of lotion out of her purse, pours some into her palm, and massages it into Barb's hands and feet. "There is a balm," Carma hums, then sings, "in Gilead, to make the wounded whole."

"I DON'T KNOW WHAT TO DO, AUNT CARMA," AMY SAYS. They lean back on a couch in the little waiting room. Carma has taken off her rocker-bottom shoes and put her feet up on the coffee table. Dan is reading to his unconscious sister. He found a copy of *Winnie the Pooh* in the gift shop. It was once her favorite book.

"That chaplain made me feel as if I were a murderer just thinking about disconnecting Mom from all that crap." Amy shakes her head. "How she'd hate it."

"She would," Carma agrees.

"And even if she gets so she can breathe on her own, with just one of those tanks—I know she'd rather die."

She didn't seem too fond of life before, Carma thinks, but doesn't say.

"She wouldn't have hesitated to pull the plug on *her* mother." Amy stops. "But she didn't have to. Even if Grandma hadn't died in the ambulance, Grandpa would've had to make the decision." She closes her eyes and breathes in. "Did Uncle Dan tell you we've decided not to tell Grandpa?"

"That's wise. He probably wouldn't remember ten minutes after. And if he did remember, he'd cry."

"They hardly even talked," Amy says. "What did he do to her anyway, to make her dislike him so much?'

Carma resettles herself on the couch. "I don't know that he did anything. But he wanted for her to come back to church."

"To be saved," Amy says.

"Well—to have a better life than she was having."

"What do you think about this being saved business?" Amy looks at her narrowly. "*You* aren't going to be saved, are you?"

"Guess not," says Carma.

"But you *live* like a Mormon," says Amy. "You don't drink alcohol, you don't even drink coffee, do you?"

"Oh," says Carma wryly, "is that what being a Mormon is?"

"Well—more than that. I guess you're supposed to go to church and to the temple."

"And believe," Carma says softly.

"Ah yes," Amy says, "and believe. Sometimes I think Mom believes—at least a little. Not the Joseph Smith thing, but at least God and Jesus and heaven. And I think she thought she was a sinner." Amy puts her feet up on the coffee table next to Carma's. "Do you think she was? And why did I just use the past tense?"

"She's not a sinner," Carma says. "I think if I believed, though, I would try to follow all the rules. I've always been in awe of people who have faith but don't follow the rules."

"If only she hadn't smoked," Amy says. "I used to tell her, 'Look, I know you won't quit for me, but how about for Buddy?' She wouldn't even quit for Buddy."

"That's the definition of addiction."

"Some addicts quit. She just gave up, caved in. Look at you— you have that awful rheumatoid arthritis, and *you* don't give up."

"It comes and goes, you know. Sometimes I want to give up."

"But you *don't.*"

"No. I guess not." But I've got a husband, Carma thinks, who really did marry me for a bit better and a lot worse. She pats Amy's hand. "Do you ever see your dad?"

Amy harrumphs. "More than she sees *her* dad. Couple times of year, something sparks his guilt, and he calls and comes up to take me out to lunch."

"He still lives here then, in Salt Lake?"

Amy nods. "Want another kid?" she asks. "I'm up for adoption."

Carma reaches over and hugs her. "We'll take you," she says.

BECAUSE BARB IS NO BETTER THE NEXT DAY, THE PROGNO-sis is worse. The machines are keeping her alive—not exactly alive, Carma thinks, but they are breathing for her and keeping her heart beating. Carma takes the elevator down and knocks on the chaplain's open door. "What right do you have," she says evenly, "to make our niece feel guilty about stopping life support?"

The chaplain looks dazed. "We just want them to see all sides," he says at last. "Her mother didn't leave very clear instructions."

"That girl," Carma says, "has been the most responsible adult in her family since she was 14." She punctuates her sentences with her cane, which seems to intimidate him. "Don't you think she knows what her mother would want? Don't you think she knows what her mother is capable of?"

He says nothing. "You talk to her again," Carma says. "You tell her you're sorry you have made her even more miserable.

You tell her that you know she loves her mother and knows what is best for her."

He apparently does it. The following day, Dan and Amy sign some papers, and Dan and the chaplain, both wearing Levi's and golf shirts, give Barb another blessing, one that thanks her for her love and her generous spirit and gives her permission to go. The moment after the nurse lifts the large oxygen tube from Barb's mouth, Barb seems to sag. She is gone. "Goodbye, Sis," Dan says, "goodbye, Beautiful," and he breaks down and weeps. Then he remembers Amy and he holds her as she sobs. Carma watches them and swallows her own tears. And Barb— she doesn't look peaceful exactly, but at least her mouth isn't all distended and sad. It wasn't that her spirit left when she died—it seemed to leave before that. It had been leaving for years maybe. What vanished was the strain—and the color in her face. Carma touches Barb's hand, already cold. She kisses Barb's cheek.

TWO OF AMY'S FRIENDS HAVE COME DOWN FROM OGDEN, Luke and Ellen—a nice young tanned couple from her hiking group. Her high school pals Susan and Jill have been waiting out in the hall. They flank Amy on the couch in the little waiting room. "What makes me feel so bad," Amy tells them, "is that the only part of her they can use is her corneas. Nothing else was good enough."

"A cornea is a huge gift if you need one," says Susan, unbuckling her sandals and settling herself into a lotus position. She smiles at Carma, sunk into an overstuffed chair by the door. Dan is out in the hall talking to Sophie on his phone.

Barb's body is to be cremated, her ashes—Amy doesn't know yet. Maybe she'll scatter them someplace, maybe Millcreek Canyon, maybe Alta. There will be a get-together, a small one, at the house. In about two weeks, or three. Dan and Carma will fly back. Barb's ski bum friends, some of her cousins from Logan, Amy's own friends will come. And Grace and Ryan. "And the kids," Amy says. "Then I can see the baby. You don't mind if I don't drive down on Sunday for that blessing ceremony? I can see Grace and the kids at the open house." Carma nods to signal of course.

What to do with the house? She'll have to decide. Buddy? "No one who knows him will want him," says Amy.

"Maybe we can donate him," Luke grins, "to a research lab."

"Craig's List," says Ellen. "We'll write a killer ad."

Susan and Jill insist Amy stay in Jill's apartment for the night, as many nights as she wants, Jill says. Amy agrees. Dan slips back into the waiting room. He reaches down into Carma's chair to lift her to her feet and puts her cane in her right hand. When Amy hugs them, her eyes fill with tears. "We'll come back tomorrow," Dan says.

JUST DAN COMES BACK. IT'S A BAD NIGHT FOR BOTH OF them, but in the morning, Carma can hardly move. Her knees and ankles throb. Dan takes her to Grace's and insists she lie down on the couch. He puts an orange afghan over her legs. Bradley sidles up to her. "Will you watch my programs with me, Gamma?"

"Sure," she says and waves goodbye to Dan. Sometimes she laughs when Bradley laughs, sometimes she hears his programs and his whining and the baby's fussing and Grace's cooing through a haze, sometimes she sleeps. "I'm sorry you feel so crummy," Grace says to Carma, "but it's great to have you here, all to myself."

Carma pushes her head up to the arm of the couch. "You're a natural mother," she says, "something I could never be."

Grace smiles. "You don't think we should postpone the blessing tomorrow, do you?"

"Of course not," Carma says. "That's what allows us to accept death. Life. Babies."

"We won't be able to think of Cammy's blessing without remembering Aunt Barb dying."

Carma sits up straighter on the couch. "We won't be able to think of Barb dying without remembering Cammy's blessing."

"Touché," says Grace.

Dan is back by supper, minestrone someone from the church made, and Carma thinks it tastes wonderful. Dan usually gives up dinner the evening before Fast Sunday, but neither he nor Ryan suggests that tonight. Carma and Dan leave early for the motel, and this night is different from all the preceding nights: they sleep.

CARMA AND DAN MEET GRACE AND RYAN AND THE KIDS AT the church—they won't all fit into either of their cars. They slide into a side pew halfway down the chapel aisle: Carma and Bradley, who has taken possession again of Carma's cane, next to the wall; the baby, now sleeping, in a ruffled carrier on the floor beside Grace. In the pew in front of them, Ryan's parents and one of his brothers and his family stand up and greet them and offer hands to shake and cheeks to kiss. "We're so sorry," Ryan's mother whispers, "about your sister." Ryan's nieces run to look at the baby. Into the pew behind them file more of Ryan's family, another brother and his brood. Everyone settles down just before the meeting begins. The opening hymn is "Master, the Tempest Is Raging." The organist misses a few chords, but the congregation enthusiastically belts out both the "Storm-tossed sea" and the "Peace, be still."

The major item of ward business, it appears, is the blessing of their baby. Grace takes sleeping Cammy out of the carrier and carefully places her in Ryan's outstretched arms. He and Dan and Ryan's father and brothers walk down the aisle to the front of the chapel, assorted men joining them from their seats in the congregation or on the stand. Carma hopes the baby stays asleep. It would be terrifying to wake up surrounded by so many big men in dark suits. It's good that Sophie is in New York. She would be outraged that Grace isn't allowed in the circle. No women. When Dan asked Sophie why she couldn't at least stay in the church until she was 21, she said, "Women aren't welcome. Women aren't important."

This isn't what went wrong for Carma. Carma doesn't remember ever wanting the priesthood that the men have, and she certainly doesn't want it now. But she has told Sophie that she believes that it would be better if everyone who wanted the priesthood could have it. "Do you want it?" she asked Sophie once. "Well, sure," Sophie had said. But Carma doesn't believe her.

Ryan begins. "By the authority," he says, "of the Holy Melchizedek Priesthood, which we hold, we give this child a name and a blessing. The name by which she shall be known on the records of the church is Camilla Barbara Gibson."

Carma jerks in her seat. She can see Dan's face, eyes shut, tears leaking out. The men's shoulders all move slightly as they bounce the sleeping baby.

Ryan says nice things about what he and Grace hope for Camilla—that she will be blessed with health—no autoimmune diseases, no addictive tendencies, thinks Carma—that she will be kind and sensitive to those around her, that she will one day find a young man worthy of her and marry in the temple and have a family of her own. Did Dan say those things when he blessed Grace and Sophie? He must have. That was some years before Carma's faith failed. And at both baby blessings, she was too sleep-deprived, too frantic, too ill to pay attention and remember.

The circle disperses, most of the men taking their seats. After Ryan holds Camilla up so the congregation can see her—white, frilly, angelic, and asleep—he struts up the aisle and lays the baby on Grace's lap and slides in next to her. Grace scoots over next to Carma and Bradley, and Dan takes the seat on the aisle. The chorister leads the congregation in the sacrament hymn. A small army of young boys in white shirts and ties carry the sacrament bread trays up the aisles. Carma doesn't take the bread even when Bradley looks questioningly at her. In—how many years?—he will be wearing a white shirt and tie and holding a stainless steel tray of bread. By then, he will perhaps understand that only one of his grandmothers is a real Mormon.

As a tall young man kneels to bless the water, Grace whispers to her mother, "That boy's autistic, but he's come a long way." Carma has already noticed him, a beautiful boy with clear, unpimpled skin and a wide cap of curly blond hair. "O God, the Eternal Father," he begins, "we ask thee in the name of thy Son, Jesus Christ, to bless and sanctify this water to the souls of all those who drink of it." Carma is startled. His voice is not the voice of a teenager mechanically reading a prayer. He is earnest, passionate. For him, it is real. ". . . in remembrance of the blood of thy Son, which was shed for them"—the boy is almost keening "that they may witness unto thee, O God, the Eternal Father . . . ." He is a witness, this boy. He's almost enough to make one believe. Carma shakes her head just a little. Almost enough, but not quite.

Ryan, then Grace, stand and talk during the testimony-bearing part of the meeting. Each expresses gratitude for the perfect baby, for Bradley, for their parents and siblings. Grace acknowledges the loss of her father's sister and says they hope to honor her and him by giving her name to Camilla. Others rise and speak. Ryan's father seems just a little pompous. A woman hiccoughs out a harrowing tale of driving down a steep hill, her baby in the carseat behind her, when the brakes went out. A voice in her ear told her to use the emergency brake. A leggy teenage girl in a very short denim skirt has to bend down to use the microphone. She loves everyone. Her ward friends are so cool.

After the closing prayer, the pews of relatives gather up children and bags, exchange pleasantries with local members in the lobby, and head out the doors. Ryan's parents are hosting a family brunch so none of the clan is staying for other meetings. Tonight, Carma and Dan will kiss Grace and Ryan and the children goodbye before the last night at the motel. Tomorrow, they will touch base with Amy and then fly back to Oakland.

At the end of the parking lot, past the rental car which Carma wouldn't let Dan park in one of the handicapped places, she spots the blonde young man who blessed the water. He stands alone, hands on hips, looking up into a tree. He has shed his suit jacket. His trousers are not quite long enough—his yellow socks an unsettling swath above his black shoes. Carma squints up at the branches that have captured his gaze, but sees nothing, nothing but leaves. Maybe that's all there is.

"Coming?" Dan asks.

She leans lightly on her cane. "Coming," she says.

About the Author

KAREN ROSENBAUM EARNED HER B.A. FROM THE UNIVERSITY of Utah and her M.A. from Stanford University under the direction of Wallace Stegner. For thirty-four years she taught at Ohlone College in Fremont, California. Her published work comprises short stories, personal essays, and newspaper articles, some of which have won awards from *Sunstone, Exponent II,* and *Dialogue: A Journal of Mormon Thought.* She has been accorded honorary lifetime membership status by the Association for Mormon Letters. She lives with her husband in Kensington, California.